Mail Order Magnate

Book 55 in Brides of Beckham

Kirsten Osbourne

Chapter One

Isabelle Winslow looked around her at the walls of Elizabeth Tandy's office. She and her sisters Anabelle and Rosabelle had buried their mother less than a week before, and they'd sneaked out of their father's home to escape his abuse just hours before.

Now, she Ana and Rosie were sitting together on the sofa in Elizabeth's office, reading letters that were from men who were looking for mail-order brides. The non-identical triplets had nowhere else to go, so they agreed to read letters from three men who were all from the same small town in Colorado, deciding if they would agree to be their mail-order brides.

Izzy read through her letter, from the mayor of Hope Springs, and she instantly knew the letter was meant for Rosie. Rosie would be a wonderful mayor's wife, and she did not incline to be the first lady of a small town. No, she wanted someone who would be able to give her whatever she needed in life, and a small-town mayor wouldn't be able to do that.

Izzy nodded, her brunette locks brushing against her cheek, but her heart hammered against her ribs like a bird in a cage. Ana's fingers twisted a strand of her fiery hair, winding and unwinding with every breath she drew. Beside them, Rosie's hands lay folded in her lap, her blonde curls cascading over her shoulders.

Izzy had always admired Rosie for being able to stay calm through any situation.

"Remember," Elizabeth said, her gaze flitting over the sisters, "this arrangement is as much about survival as it is about matrimony. It's a harsh world out there for women alone. And though you wouldn't be

"

able to live together, at least you would be in the same town, and be able to spend time together.

"Your lives are about to change," Elizabeth said softly, "one way or another."

Izzy carefully read the letter that had been handed to Rosie.

April 1898

Dearest Prospective Companion,

My name is Albert Thoreau, a name perhaps whispered on the winds of this mining town for the silver veins I've been blessed to uncover beneath its rugged beauty. Yet, amidst the wealth and wonders, I am alone.

Hope Springs is a town that thrives not just on the bounty beneath the ground, but on the spirit of community, the warmth of shared endeavors, and the quiet strength that binds us. It is here that I've built a life marked by material success. Yet as I enjoy the wealth my good fortune has brought me, I find that it's hard to truly be happy while I am alone.

I seek not just a wife, but a true partner—to share in the joys and challenges that life in Hope Springs presents. A woman whose eyes sparkle with curiosity and kindness, whose laughter is a melody that brightens the darkest of days, and whose presence turns a house into a home.

In you, I seek a companion to explore not only the beauty of this world but the depths of our own spirits. A woman who values the richness of the heart above the glitter of gold, who sees in every day an opportunity for love, learning, and laughter. Together, I believe we can build a life that transcends the ordinary—a partnership based on mutual respect, deep affection, and an unwavering commitment to each other's growth and happiness.

If these words stir something within you, then I eagerly await your reply. Let us take the first tentative steps toward a future filled with the light of understanding and the warmth of companionship.

With a hopeful heart,

Mr. Albert Thoreau

Hope Springs, Colorado

As the silence settled once more, Izzy's spine stiffened. She would go west and marry this man, not as a victim of circumstance, but as the architect of her own destiny.

Izzy's gaze returned to the letter, to Albert's promises of partnership. He would suit her much better than a mayor would, and if she and her sisters went to the same small town, they would still be together. She had never spent a night without her sisters. She'd rarely spent an hour without both of them at her side, and she didn't want to start now.

"I'll marry this man," Izzy declared.

IZZY AND ROSIE CLASPED their hands tightly as if their joined fingers could ward off the uncertainty that clawed at their bellies. Ana sat opposite them as Beckham disappeared. The world outside blurred past them, a mosaic of colors streaking by as the locomotive devoured the miles toward Hope Springs.

"Remember," Ana whispered, her voice a thin thread of sound barely heard above the din, "no matter what happens, we're in this together."

Rosie gave a small nod, her eyes rimmed with fear she couldn't voice.

Izzy's gaze drifted to the window, where her reflection stared back at her—a ghostly specter framed by the sweeping landscape. The countryside was a vast expanse of muted greens and browns, the distant mountains a jagged line against the sky.

The train lurched into the station with a hiss of steam and a screech of metal on metal, jolting Izzy from her thoughts. Her sisters rose with her, the three of them swaying slightly as they gathered their meager belongings. They stepped onto the platform.

Izzy's breath hitched in her throat as she scanned the sea of faces, searching for the man who held her future in his hands. Albert Thoreau—the name was a talisman she turned over in her mind.

"Perhaps they're not here yet," Rosie murmured, trying to mask her disappointment with a hopeful lilt.

As they waited, all three holding hands, Dr. Mercer—the man Ana was marrying came forward and took Ana away after a short introduction. The man looked too serious to Izzy, and she hoped her sister would get along well with him. As Ana walked away, Izzy looked over at Rosie. "I don't know when we'll see her again. Have we made a terrible mistake?"

Rosie squeezed the hand she was holding. "It will all be fine. I'm sure of it."

But Izzy wasn't like her sister. Rosie always wore rose-colored glasses. Even when their father had beaten her, she'd always come up with reasons why he was the way he was.

"Stay close," she instructed her sister, her voice betraying none of the tremor that threatened to undo her.

And then, the crowd parted, and there he was. Even from a distance, she recognized him—the embodiment of influence and affluence. "I believe that's Albert coming toward us," Izzy whispered.

"Isabelle?" His voice cut through the clamor, clear and authoritative, reaching her like a lifeline—or a leash.

"Mr. Thoreau," Izzy replied, her words measured, her tone respectful but devoid of warmth. "My family calls me Izzy."

"Then I shall call you that as well. And you must call me Albert." He looked at her carefully. "Who is this?"

Izzy smiled. "This is my sister Rosabelle, whom we call Rosie."

"It's nice to meet you," he said. His eyes swept over her. In that moment, Izzy understood that she was not merely a bride. She was an acquisition. "Welcome to Hope Springs."

"Thank you," Izzy replied, placing her hand in his with deliberate care. She turned to embrace Rosie, not knowing when she would see either of her sisters again.

She would endure. She would adapt. With one last glance at her sister, Isabelle squared her shoulders and walked alongside Albert Thoreau.

"We will go to church and marry. And then I'll take you to my home and introduce you to my housekeeper, who will help you with whatever you need."

"Of course," Izzy said. She hadn't considered she would have a housekeeper. It would feel odd not to do everything herself. She wasn't yet certain what to think of Albert, but at least he'd been prompt in retrieving her from the train station. That was a mark in his favor. Though he did seem to be a bit too fussy with his appearance, his suit was perfect.

She knew the world was ruled by men like Albert Thoreau, but she would not let it snuff out the fire of her spirit. She was a fixture in his plan, yes, but not an inert one. She would learn, she would observe, and she would find a way to claim her place within this new life.

"Shall we?" Albert finally said, glancing back at her with an unreadable expression as they reached the end of the platform, the beginning of everything else.

"Let's go," Izzy affirmed.

The wedding was a brisk affair as if it were another transaction in Albert Thoreau's ledger. As she stood beside him, clad in one of the two dresses she'd left her father's house with, she hoped that life with him wouldn't be anything like life with her father. She wouldn't stay if he was violent. She simply couldn't spend the rest of her life the way she'd spent it so far.

"Isabelle Grace," the officiant intoned. "Do you take this man to be your lawfully wedded husband?"

Her answer was a faint, "I do." No matter how nervous she was, she'd agreed to marry this man. Albert's response mirrored hers in volume, though devoid of any detectable emotion.

The officiant pronounced them man and wife in a voice devoid of warmth, and as tradition dictated, Albert leaned down to bestow upon Izzy a quick kiss. His lips brushed against hers—a fleeting contact that left no impression of tenderness or promise. It was perfunctory. Izzy hoped he didn't do everything that way.

THE GRANDEUR OF ALBERT Thoreau's house loomed before Izzy as they approached, its towering presence a stark reminder of the life she was now bound to. She gazed up at the imposing structure. It was perfect. She only hoped he didn't expect her to be just as perfect.

"Welcome to your new home, Mrs. Thoreau," Albert said. There was no warmth in the welcome, no guiding hand at her back—only the expectation that she would step into the role she'd been given.

"Thank you," Izzy managed. She couldn't shake the feeling of being an outsider, a stranger stepping into a play halfway through, the script long since written without her input.

As the door creaked open, revealing the cavernous foyer within, Izzy realized that this house was not a home but a fortress. And she, merely a silent figure moving through its halls, searching for a foothold in a world where she had yet to find her place.

"Shall we discuss the arrangements?" Albert's voice was devoid of inflection as if he were inquiring about the weather rather than their shared life.

"Of course," she replied, her tone equally measured. It would help to know exactly what he expected of her.

They settled into an ornate sitting room where the plush furniture seemed to mock her discomfort. Izzy perched on the edge of a velvet armchair. She folded her hands in her lap, clenching them tightly, so he wouldn't see they were trembling.

"Your duties will be clear," Albert began. "You will manage the household, host my business associates, and attend social functions as befits my status."

"Understood," Izzy responded. She could feel the walls of the house closing in around her.

"Children," Albert continued, glancing up for the first time, his green eyes probing, "are expected promptly."

Izzy nodded, her throat tight as she acknowledged the demand. She had thought to ask him to postpone the wedding night, but it was apparent that wasn't going to happen. "Is there anything else you require from me?" Izzy asked.

"Simply your compliance," he replied. There was no malice in his voice, only the cold clarity of a man who viewed his new wife as part of his empire.

"Then you shall have it," Izzy said, her words clipped, yet her gaze unwavering. She would carve out a place for herself.

"Very well." Albert folded the document with a crisp snap, signaling the end of their negotiation. As he rose, he extended a hand toward her—not in comfort, but as a formality, a conclusion to their bargain.

"Welcome to our partnership, Mrs. Thoreau," he said, and Izzy accepted his hand.

"Thank you, Mr. Thoreau," she replied, her fingers brushing against his palm briefly before withdrawing. It felt odd to be so formal with her husband, but it seemed to be what he desired.

As Albert exited the room, leaving her alone amid the opulence, Izzy allowed herself a single, shuddering breath. She rose from the armchair, her every step a quiet declaration of her intent to endure, to adapt, to survive.

Izzy's heels clicked against the polished floors of the grand foyer as she trailed behind Albert.

"Every worthwhile venture in town bears my mark. The lumber mill, the general store, even the saloon—they all feed into the Thoreau legacy," he said, a hint of pride lacing his tone.

"Quite the empire," Izzy murmured, her gaze drifting toward the window where the town lay spread out beneath them.

"Yes, it is," he replied, oblivious to the churn of her thoughts. "And I expect you to uphold my reputation. A Thoreau wife must be beyond reproach."

His words were cold and factual. Izzy felt the tightening grip of the golden cage, its bars invisible yet unyielding.

"Of course, Mr. Thoreau," she said, her voice steady despite the turmoil that brewed within her.

As Albert left the house, Izzy kept exploring. She finally found the kitchen and spotted a woman there, stirring a pot of something on the stove. "Hello. I'm Izzy," she said softly.

"Mrs. Thoreau. Welcome. I'm the housekeeper here. My name is Martha Kirkland." Martha had gray hair and looked to be around her parents' age. She was thick around the middle and had a kind look about her.

Izzy smiled, taking an apron off a hook on the wall. "What can I do to help with supper?"

Martha's eyes widened. "Absolutely nothing. It's my job to cook, and it's your job to tell me what to cook."

Izzy shook her head. "I can't. I don't have any idea what to tell anyone to cook. I'm afraid I was raised in a household where I only saw my sisters and my parents every day. I need to learn what people do."

Martha smiled. "I understand. I'll teach you as much as I can. Did you mention to Mr. Thoreau that you don't know how to manage a household?"

Izzy shook her head. "No, I didn't, and I would prefer he not know that I'm lacking in that area."

"Then we'll start your lessons now, while he's out of the house." Martha smiled sweetly. "There's so much to teach you, and I can't wait to get started. There are no dinner parties for more than a week, so there's time." Martha looked at Izzy's dress. "You'll need new clothes."

Izzy nodded. "I can make myself a new dress."

Martha laughed softly. "Oh, honey. You need at least a dozen new dresses. Make one for yourself but let me get a dressmaker in here Monday morning to meet with you."

"That would help me a great deal!" Izzy said, smiling. "I'm glad I found you."

"Well, I'm old enough to be your mother, so if you don't mind, I'll treat you like I would treat a daughter."

"Nothing could make me happier." Izzy was thrilled that Martha seemed to understand all she needed to learn. Thank heavens. Disappointing Albert was not something she wanted to do.

Chapter Two

Izzy's fingers hesitated over the dough. The kitchen, with its gleaming copper pots and well-worn wooden table, was Martha's domain, a place of savory aromas and simmering pots that Izzy now needed to navigate as part of her wifely duties. Ana had been more interested in cooking than Izzy had been, so she felt a bit inept in the kitchen.

"Albert likes his bread to have a firm crust," Martha said, her voice carrying the weight of authority as she guided Izzy's hands with her own. "He expects his meals to be on time and his house to be spotless."

The air was thick with the heat from the oven, and Izzy could feel a bead of sweat trail down her spine. She nodded, committing Martha's words to memory while kneading the dough with more conviction, trying to find some semblance of control in the situation she found herself in.

"Does he ever speak of...affection?" Izzy ventured, her heart fluttering with hope.

"Affection is a luxury," Martha replied curtly, her eyes never leaving the task at hand. "Albert Thoreau is a man of business. He respects efficiency and obedience above all else."

The room seemed to close in around Izzy. She realized that in this house, emotions were burdensome. Her role as Albert's wife was one of function, not of love or partnership. She wanted things to be different, and she would just have to bide her time. Oh, how she wished she had Rosie's ability to be patient.

"Come now," Martha said after a period of heavy silence, wiping her hands on her apron. "I'll show you to your bedroom."

They ascended the creaky staircase, each step a reminder of the permanence of Izzy's decision. When they reached the door at the end, Martha pushed it open to reveal the marital chamber.

It was a large room, dominated by a massive four-poster bed draped in heavy fabrics. The windows were draped in dark curtains, muting the sunlight, and casting a gloom over the ornate furniture.

As she looked around her, she realized that she would have preferred bright colors. She wondered how Albert would feel if she were to change things.

"Albert will expect you to be ready when he retires for the evening," Martha stated plainly, pulling back the quilt to expose the crisp white sheets beneath. "He does not tolerate tardiness or indecision."

Izzy felt the weight of expectation bearing down upon her. The room, which should have been a sanctuary, now felt like a cage. The reality of sharing this intimate space with a man she hardly knew—a man who saw her as little more than property—settled in her stomach like a stone.

"Thank you, Martha," Izzy managed to say.

"Good," Martha nodded once, approval and pity mingling in her gaze. "I'll leave you to get acquainted with your duties. Supper will be served promptly at six."

With that, Martha left. Alone in the looming shadow of the marriage bed, Izzy's resolve wavered. She would have to learn quickly, adapt to Albert's expectations, or be swallowed whole by the bleak existence that stretched out before her.

Izzy's fingers brushed over the worn fabric of her small satchel, its contents meager and unassuming. One by one, she lifted her belongings—a pair of threadbare stockings, a comb with several teeth missing, and a modest cotton dress—and nestled them into the ornate dresser that seemed to mock her simplicity.

With a sigh, she withdrew the last item, her plain white nightgown, holding it up against her frame. The material was soft from wear, comforting in its familiarity, yet as she eyed the magnificent bed, she couldn't help but feel a pang of longing for something more refined, something delicate and laced with the promise of romance. This was, after all, her wedding night, wasn't it? Yet the thought brought a bitter taste to her mouth.

"Should've had a pretty nightdress," she murmured to herself. The gown fell from her hands, folding obediently into the final drawer, an acceptance of sorts.

Drawn as if by some invisible force, Izzy approached the window, her movements slow. Her hands pulled aside the dark curtains. She peered down at the town of Hope Springs.

The roofs of buildings dotted the view, each sheltering lives and stories she might never know. Somewhere down there, perhaps, her sisters were with their new husbands and seeing their new homes. Were they gazing out of their windows too, yearning for a connection severed by distance and fate?

"Anabelle...Rosabelle..." she whispered their names, a silent prayer for their well-being. A tightness gripped her chest—a blend of worry and solitude—as she pondered their fates. Were they safe? Content? Did they, too, lay out their nightgowns with trembling hands?

A cool breeze wafted through the open pane, carrying with it the faint sounds of life outside. Life moved on, relentless and indifferent to the stillness that had settled upon Izzy's shoulders.

Her gaze lingered on the horizon, where the mountains stood. Perhaps, in their ancient wisdom, they held the answers to the questions that plagued her heart. For now, though, those answers remained as elusive as the touch of warmth she so desperately sought in this new existence.

THE CLINK OF CUTLERY on fine china punctuated the silence that had fallen over the dining room. Albert sat rigidly at the head of the long mahogany table, his posture an unspoken decree of authority.

At the opposite end of the table, Izzy perched, a lone figure dwarfed by the expanse between them. She felt every inch the accessory in his perfect vision of domesticity. Martha's footsteps were soft as she moved about the room, serving up portions with deference and precision. The housekeeper's presence was the only warmth in the vast, ornate space, yet it did nothing to temper the chill of the arrangement.

Izzy lifted her fork, the weight of it unfamiliar in her hand, like so many things in this new life. Across from her, Albert's jaw worked methodically, his eyes never leaving his plate, the embodiment of detachment.

The meal concluded with mechanical finality. Albert wiped his mouth with a linen napkin, pushed his chair back, and stood. Without a word or a glance toward Izzy, he departed the room. He retreated to his office—the inner sanctum where his true passions lay.

Left in the wake of his absence, Izzy rose and gathered the dishes with quiet resignation. She carried them to the kitchen, where Martha waited with the sink filled with steaming water. The clatter of porcelain being submerged broke the oppressive stillness, the suds caressing Izzy's hands like a consoling touch.

"Let me help you," Izzy said, rolling up her sleeves despite the lingering scent of roast beef and the quiet protest of her aching muscles.

Martha offered a small smile, lines of kindness etched into her weathered face. "You needn't trouble yourself, Mrs. Thoreau. This is my duty."

"Please," Izzy insisted, "I can't sit still. I need to do something with my hands." It was a plea for normalcy in a world where she felt utterly adrift.

Together they worked, the scrape of plates and the slosh of water filling the void left by Albert's departure. Izzy washed while Martha dried. For a fleeting moment, there was camaraderie in the task, a shared burden in a house where Izzy hoped she would one day feel at home.

"Thank you," Izzy whispered as she handed a rinsed platter to Martha.

Martha nodded, accepting the dish and the gratitude with equal grace. "We look after our own here," she said, though her eyes betrayed the knowledge that within these walls, some were more alone than others.

As they finished, the kitchen regained its order, but the silence lingered—a reminder that peace was merely an illusion in the shadow of Albert Thoreau's will.

Izzy lingered by the sink, her fingers tracing the cold edge as she gazed through the window.

"Mrs. Thoreau," Martha began. "You oughtn't be here scrubbing away. A woman of your standing should spend her evenings with needlework or a book. That's what Mr. Thoreau would expect."

"Expect?" Izzy's gaze snapped from the window to Martha. As much as she wanted to please her husband, she refused to bend her will to be what any man wanted. "I'm no porcelain doll to sit pretty and idle." Her hands clenched, the skin chafed from the dishwater.

Martha's look was one of sympathy muddled with caution. "It ain't about what we find, but what is given," she murmured, her eyes flitting to the grandfather clock in the corner of the room.

As if summoned by the ticking of time, Albert's voice cut through the air like the final toll of the hour. "Isabelle, it is time." His words were clipped, precise, devoid of warmth. "Prepare yourself for bed. I will join you shortly."

The command hung heavy in the room, an unyielding decree that brooked no opposition. Izzy felt the walls close in, her newfound defiance crumbling to resignation. She gave Martha a terse nod, her footsteps muted against the wooden floor as she retreated from the kitchen, each step a resignation to the order of her world.

Izzy's fingers fumbled with the buttons of her dress, a cascade of fabric pooling at her feet. She pulled the plain white nightgown over her head, its cotton whispering against her skin. It hung on her frame, unadorned and functional, as if to mirror the stark transaction her life had become.

She slid between the stiff sheets, the chill linen pressing against her legs. Her limbs were rigid, arranging themselves in careful symmetry, a ritual of compliance she had yet to understand but felt compelled to perform. The nightgown seemed to leech the warmth from her skin.

Footsteps echoed up the staircase, deliberate and unhurried. The door creaked open, a sliver of light slicing through the darkness before being extinguished by him.

Albert shed his clothes with the same mechanical precision that he seemed to do everything with.

The bed dipped beneath his weight, the springs protesting with a faint groan as he settled beside her. Izzy's breath hitched, a silent gasp swallowed by the void between them. His body exuded a heat that was the complete opposite of the coldness of his demeanor.

There was no word, no glance of acknowledgment as he lay there, an unbreachable distance measured in inches. Izzy's eyes traced the profile of his face, wanting to see some sort of emotion, but there was none there.

Albert shifted, his movements deliberate and sure. Izzy tensed, unsure of what his touch would bring. She knew the mechanics of what to expect, but she had no idea how it would feel to have him touch her.

She felt his hand, an unexpected warmth against the cool expanse of her skin, a contradiction to the aloofness that clung to him.

His touch was not the perfunctory gesture she had braced herself for but rather a careful exploration that kindled a flicker of something forbidden within her—a desire she could scarcely name. Izzy's breath caught as he drew nearer, the space between them collapsing into a tangle of limbs and whispered sighs.

Albert transformed beneath the veil of darkness. His lips found hers with an urgency that surprised her. He moved with a fervor that spoke of hidden depths, a passion that danced on the edge of ferocity, yet tempered by a gentleness that cradled her in its embrace.

Izzy's world, which had been painted in shades of duty and decorum, burst into vivid color at his ministrations. Her own body responded in kind, moving against him with an innate rhythm that surprised her as much as it seemed to delight him. The sensation of being truly seen left her breathless.

For those fleeting moments, as they moved together in the silent symphony of their union, Izzy forgot the cold pragmatism of their arrangement. She was no longer just the wife of Albert Thoreau, the businessman. Instead, she felt as if she was awakened by his touch, much as Sleeping Beauty had been woken by the kiss of the prince.

"Well, that was unexpectedly fun," she said, grinning at him in the darkness.

He chuckled. "I hope you always feel that way."

But as quickly as the flame had ignited, it was extinguished. Albert's breaths slowed, his energy spent, and he turned from her without a word. The warmth of his body moved from her, and he rolled to his side to sleep, facing away from her.

Izzy lay there, the echoes of pleasure still thrumming through her, as Albert's steady breathing told her he was asleep. There was a haunting solitude that crept over her. She had never slept alone, and even though she wasn't alone then, she felt as if she was. She wanted things to be as they were. She wanted to still share a bed with her two sisters.

Staring up at the ceiling, Izzy grappled with the enigma that was her husband. How could one man house two completely different personalities—the iron-fisted ruler of an empire by day, and the fervent lover by night? Was this passion merely another facet of his ownership, or did it hint at some deeper well of emotion yet untapped?

Her heart ached in the silence that followed, yearning for a sign that what passed between them had meant something more than physical satiation. But the answer, much like the man beside her, remained a mystery. And Izzy, lost in the immensity of her thoughts, awaited the dawn with a heavy sense of longing for what might never be.

But she would work toward it. She wasn't going to have a marriage like her mother's where her father reigned supreme and commanded all who were around him.

Chapter Three

It was past dawn when Izzy stirred from her slumber. She lay still for a moment before she pushed off the heavy quilts and slipped from the bed. The wooden floorboards were chilled against her bare feet as she padded toward the dining room where Albert was already seated at the head of the breakfast table.

"Good morning," she murmured.

Albert glanced up from his plate, his eyes trailing over her modest attire with a hint of disapproval. "Morning, Izzy," he said. "We'll be attending church today. You should wear your best dress."

Izzy's hands smoothed out the wrinkles in the simple cotton fabric that draped her frame. She met his gaze, her voice steady even as it betrayed her vulnerability. "This *is* my best dress, Albert."

Silence swathed them like a shroud. Albert's expression morphed into one of shock, his brows arching high above the rim of his spectacles. For a drawn-out moment, he scrutinized her, as if seeing her for the first time, and then a curt nod broke the tension. "That's a pity," he said.

"I'll make a new one as soon as I can," she said, her gaze meeting his without flinching.

"See that you do. Anything is better than what you're wearing."

Later, Izzy stepped through the threshold of the church, remembering little about going to church before her father had forced them to stop. She had no idea where to sit or how to behave. Her mother had taught them to pray, and she'd even assigned them scriptures to memorize as part of their learning, but Izzy remembered nothing about being in a church beyond her recent wedding ceremony that had been anything but ceremonious.

Then, through all the people gathered there, Izzy spotted her sister. Rosie's smile beckoned her. Izzy hurried toward her. They collided in an embrace that to observers looked as if they'd been apart for years.

"Rosie," Izzy whispered. "It's so good to see your face!"

"Izzy," Rosie said. "How do you like married life?"

A shadow flitted across Izzy's features. She glanced back at where Albert stood. "It is...as expected," she replied. Izzy didn't want her sisters to worry about her, and they would be concerned if they knew what a cold man Albert was.

They exchanged pleasantries. Rosie wore contentment like a second skin, speaking fondly of her husband. Yet Izzy merely nodded along, refusing to mention the chill of Albert's indifference.

Just before the service started, Ana materialized beside them. They exchanged greetings as they embraced all together.

They met up again after the service, and along with their men, they drifted toward the modest restaurant at the edge of town.

The meal was strange to Izzy, who had never been in a restaurant before. The men exchanging tales of commerce and the happenings in Hope Springs, while the women's voices wove a softer counterpoint. Albert's baritone threaded through the conversation while Izzy's contributions were but whispers. There was a symmetry to this tableau, each couple a mirror of tradition and propriety.

Izzy's gaze lingered on the cheer in her sisters' eyes, a contrast to the restraint in her own. Not for the first time, she pondered the value of silence.

Izzy lingered outside the restaurant. Rosie and Ana were beside her, their faces aglow with the prospect of an afternoon spent away from the watchful eyes of their husbands.

"Let's meet at the general store," Ana suggested, her voice tinged with a mirth that made the air around them lighter. "I've been itching to make a new dress. I felt underdressed at church this morning."

"Agreed," said Rosie. "We'll have our very own dressmaking soiree!"

Izzy smiled. "That sounds lovely." Her mind wandered to the bolts of fabric that awaited them, colors and textures that promised creation. Never before had any of the sisters been allowed to choose fabric for their own dress, and the idea was exciting.

"Shall we say this time tomorrow?" Ana's words cut through the quiet that had settled between them.

"That sounds wonderful," Izzy confirmed, the promise of sisterly companionship lifting her spirits for the first time since the vows had been spoken.

As they dispersed, each to their respective abodes, Izzy felt the weight of Albert's wealth like a chain around her neck. She didn't want her sisters to think she was better than them for having more money. In silence, there was equality. In pretense, there was kinship.

And so, as she walked alongside Albert, Izzy clung to the notion of simple pleasures—a spool of thread, a yard of cotton, a pattern sketched on brown paper. These were things she could share with her sisters, things that did not scream of silver, of mines, and of wealth untold.

"Are you well, my dear?" Albert asked, his voice cutting through her thoughts.

"Quite well," she lied smoothly. "I am looking forward to tomorrow afternoon. I'm meeting my sisters, and we're going to choose fabric for dresses."

"Good," he said. "You all need new dresses. I'm surprised the matchmaker let you come in such rags."

Izzy held on to the image of the general store, to the thought of threading needles and shaping garments. With her sisters beside her, she could pretend that all was well.

Though she didn't like what he was saying about her dress, she knew that he was right. She did look ridiculous in her threadbare garments. She'd be happy when she was dressed in a way that pleased him.

"Isabelle," Albert began, his voice devoid of warmth, "I've decided we shall spend our Sunday afternoons together. It seems only fitting, given that my weeks are consumed by the businesses."

She turned to face him, noting the stern set of his jaw, the rigid stance of authority that he wore as comfortably as his tailored suit. "I would like that, Albert," she replied, careful not to betray the fluttering in her chest at the thought of more time spent in his presence.

"Furthermore," he continued, casting a critical eye over her modest attire, "it's high time you dress in a manner befitting my wife. You shall have new dresses made."

Izzy felt a tightness grip her throat. The prospect of fine gowns filled her with dread, for they would become yet another wall between her and her sisters. "There's no need for finery," she said quietly.

"Need has nothing to do with it," he retorted sharply. "It is about appearance, about status. People must see you and know immediately who you belong to."

"Of course, Albert," she agreed, wishing she still felt as free as she had on the night she and her sisters had escaped their father's home.

Albert's gaze softened ever so slightly as he seemed to recall a time long past. "You know, Isabel, I haven't been down in the mines for over ten years now. Those days were dark. But it was down there I learned the value of hard work and persistence."

She listened, the bleakness of her new reality settling upon her as he spoke of his ascent from the bowels of the earth to the richest man in town.

"Hard work," she said. For all his talk of toil, he seemed oblivious to the notion that perhaps she yearned for something other than riches.

"Yes," he said, his attention already waning as he glanced toward the clock. "I must attend to some correspondence before supper. See to it that you speak with the dressmaker this week."

"Very well," she answered. "But didn't you want to spend Sunday afternoons together?"

"We'll start next week," he said, already down the hall and at the door of his office.

IZZY STARED ACROSS the dining table at Albert, surprised at the simple fare Martha had prepared. Fork in hand, she picked at her food, the roast chicken and root vegetables mere shapes on her plate.

"Tell me about your childhood," Albert said suddenly.

She swallowed hard, the memories of her youth surfacing like specters from a shadowy past. "I was raised alongside Anabelle and Rosabelle," she began, her voice steady despite the tremor she felt inside. "As triplets we were inseparable. I'm glad we aren't identical though."

Albert nodded, his eyes holding hers, urging her to continue.

"Father...Father was a man of iron will and stern convictions." Izzy hesitated. "He believed the world outside was no place for his daughters. After our fifth birthday, our home became our universe—our prison."

"Prison?"

"I don't know what else we would call it," Izzy said. "We were tutored within those walls by our mother without Father's knowledge. Cooking, housework, and needlework are all things we were taught. We knew nothing of boys or games, or the freedoms enjoyed by others."

Albert's brow furrowed as he absorbed her words, the lines etched deeply upon his face. "I see," he said after a moment.

The conversation lapsed once more into silence. Each bite Izzy took felt laborious, the food tasteless against her tongue. She wondered if Albert could sense the weight of her past.

"Your father's influence seems to have been quite...profound," Albert observed quietly, his gaze never leaving her face.

"Profound, yes," Izzy agreed, the word tasting like ash. "But not nurturing. Not kind."

Albert reached for his glass. "I understand," he said in a low voice, setting the glass down with a gentle thud.

Supper continued, each mouthful and movement deliberate, methodical. As the meal ended, Izzy couldn't help but feel that in this grand house, under the watchful eye of her husband, she was still caged. Imprisoned. She'd left one jail for another.

The remnants of supper lay abandoned on the dining table. Albert pushed his chair back, the sound jarring in the stillness, and excused himself with a curt nod. The door to his office closed with a soft click, leaving Izzy alone, the opulence suddenly suffocating.

She wandered through the corridors, her steps muted by the thick carpets, until she reached the sanctuary of the library. Books lined the shelves, their spines a mosaic of leather and gold leaf. Izzy's fingers traced the embossed titles, seeking solace in the tactile connection to worlds penned and bound. She selected a volume, its cover worn from use, and settled into an armchair by the fireplace.

The printed words danced before her eyes, tales of love and adventure that seemed alien to her existence. Reading felt indulgent—her hands idle when they should be busy with the labor of living. Yet she knew Albert preferred her this way.

Izzy allowed herself to be drawn into the narrative. For a brief moment, she escaped the confines of her gilded cage, her spirit soaring on the wings of fiction.

Time passed unnoticed until Albert appeared at the doorway. "Isabelle," he called, his voice void of the day's distance.

"Albert," she responded, marking her place with a ribbon and closing the book. She rose to meet him, the book clasped like a shield against her chest.

In the privacy of their chamber, the air shifted, charged with an intimacy that only nightfall could bring. As Albert's hands undressed her, Izzy marveled at his transformation. With each touch, each kiss, the walls he built around himself crumbled into dust.

Here, in the tangle of sheets and the mingling of breaths, they were equals. His caresses spoke louder than any words could—you are wanted, you are seen—and for a fleeting second, the powerlessness that shadowed her days receded into the darkness.

As they moved together, a rhythm as old as time itself, Izzy clung to the revelation that in the vulnerability of their union, all pretenses fell away. This was her favorite time of day, not because of passion's flame, but because here, entwined with Albert, she glimpsed the man behind the mask.

Afterward, as he lay beside her, his breathing deep and even, Izzy traced the lines of his face with her eyes, memorizing the contours softened by sleep. Even now, with his defenses laid bare, she sensed the weight of the world he carried, the expectations of a society that demanded strength and silence from its men.

Izzy turned her gaze toward the window. She sought the promise of tomorrow, a hope that maybe, just maybe, the walls between them might one day remain nothing but rubble.

Chapter Four

Shortly after breakfast the following morning a knock echoed through the quiet house, signaling the arrival of the modiste. Izzy descended the staircase with deliberate steps.

"Mrs. Thoreau," the modiste greeted with a practiced smile, unfurling an array of sketches onto the dining table like a deck of possibilities fanned out in front of her. The scent of fresh ink and parchment mingled with the musty air, and Izzy's fingers trembled slightly as she reached out to touch the first sketch.

"Good morning," Izzy replied. She studied each drawing with a critical eye, noting the fine lines that depicted silhouettes more suited for high society than the rugged edges of the frontier. Swaths of fabric in rich colors and sumptuous textures were laid before her, each one promising transformation.

For hours, Izzy went through the motions, selecting trims and buttons, lace and ribbons, while the modiste watched with a keen gaze. The six dresses she chose—one for each day of the week, save Sunday—were a study in modest elegance. A dove gray for Monday, a gentle blue for Tuesday, all the way to a soft green for Saturday. Each one was chosen not only for its appearance but for its ability to please Albert.

"Mr. Thoreau will be most satisfied with your choices, Mrs. Thoreau. These are practical and becoming," the modiste remarked.

"Thank you," Izzy murmured, folding her hands in her lap to still their quivering. It was more than just dresses she was choosing—it was a uniform to display her husband's wealth and status. Yet beneath the layers of impending silk and satin, a quiet rebellion simmered within her.

"Mrs. Thoreau," the dressmaker began, her voice carrying an edge of obligation, "your husband has instructed me to create fifteen dresses for you."

The number echoed in Izzy's ears, amplifying until it filled the room with its absurdity. Fifteen dresses was a ridiculous number. She had never had more than two at a time in her life!

"Surely, there's been some mistake," Izzy replied. Her gaze dropped to the sketches, now a clutter of excess and expectation. "Six should suffice. One for each day of the week when you include the one I'm wearing."

"Mr. Thoreau was explicit." The dressmaker met Izzy's eyes. "He desires his wife to be a reflection of his prosperity. Fifteen dresses, no less. And you'll need some that are much grander than those you've chosen. Those are suitable for every day, but you'll need evening gowns and dresses to wear when entertaining."

Izzy felt the weight of them. She drew a breath. "It's too much," she said. "I cannot..."

But the protest withered under the dressmaker's scrutiny. Izzy knew it was not a question of can or cannot, but a matter of will or will not.

The dressmaker's fingers paused over the unfolded bolt of silk, her question slicing through the silence. "Shall I select the remaining gowns, Mrs. Thoreau?"

Izzy's hands lay still in her lap, the swatches of fabric beneath them a riot of colors she couldn't bring herself to care for.

"Mrs. Thoreau?" The dressmaker prompted again.

"Very well," Izzy conceded, her voice barely a murmur as she acquiesced to the unspoken command behind the request. Each word felt like it was leading her somewhere she didn't want to go.

As the dressmaker flipped through the sketches with renewed vigor, Izzy watched the parade of potential dresses. A frill here, a ribbon there—all garnishes on a life that was being served to her by someone else's hand. With each selection, she felt taunted by the frivolity of it all. What would her sisters think?

"Perhaps this one," the dressmaker proposed, holding up a drawing of a gown with intricate beading along the bodice.

Izzy nodded, the motion. What did it matter if she wore six dresses or sixteen? They were all costumes in a play where she had no say in the script.

"Or this, with the lace overlay," the dressmaker continued, oblivious to the struggle that played out across Izzy's features.

"Fine," Izzy agreed again, each affirmation sticking in her throat. She was constructing her own cage with these ridiculous garments. Why had she thought she wanted to marry a wealthy man?

The dressmaker beamed, content with the progress, while Izzy's smile was empty. She rose, her movements stiff and robotic. She had no doubt the dressmaker would follow her husbands instructions, and it didn't really matter what she said and wanted.

IZZY SAT ACROSS FROM Albert at the lunch table, her hands folded neatly in her lap atop the fine linen tablecloth. Sunlight streamed through the window, casting a warm glow on the elaborate spread of dishes that Martha had prepared. The aroma of roasted chicken mingled with the fresh scent of baked bread, but the richness of the feast did nothing to ease the tightness in Izzy's chest.

"Everything is delicious, Martha outdid herself again," Albert remarked, his voice carrying an air of casual satisfaction as he sampled a forkful of greens.

"Yes," Izzy murmured, her own food untouched. Guilt gnawed at her. She should have been by Martha's side, contributing to the household, instead of drowning in a sea of silk and taffeta.

"Is everything to your liking, Izzy?" Albert's gaze was sharp, like a hawk surveying its domain.

"Of course," she lied, pushing around the glazed carrots on her plate. "I spent the morning choosing dresses and gowns. I think fifteen new dresses is too many."

Albert frowned. "It's important for my wife to present herself well."

"Six would have been plenty," she said more to herself than to him.

"More is better," he replied curtly, dismissing her sentiment as though swatting away an irritating fly.

"Later today," Izzy ventured, desperate to change the subject, "I am meeting Ana and Rosie at the general store. We're to select fabrics for new dresses. We want to work on them together."

"You will enjoy that," Albert said dryly. "I do hope that you will all choose something appropriate."

"Of course," Izzy assured him.

"Make sure you return before supper," he instructed.

"Absolutely," she replied, her acquiescence automatic, the dutiful words of a woman well-versed in obedience.

As lunch concluded, Izzy excused herself, her movements stiff and deliberate. She longed for the simplicity of flour-stained aprons and the honest work of kneading dough, but she must live in her husband's world.

"Isabelle," he called, a command veiled as an invitation. She paused, turning slightly, her posture taut with anticipation. "Remember, you needn't worry about the cost at Watson's General Store. I have an account there. Charge anything that suits your fancy."

"Thank you, Albert," Izzy replied. She watched his figure retreat into the cool darkness of the house. It felt good to be able to walk around town on her own, something she'd never experienced before. Soon, she and her sisters would have time together, and she couldn't wait.

The walk to the general store was a taste of autonomy as she navigated the streets of Hope Springs. She passed women in aprons, men tipping hats, and children playing with hoops, all under the watchful eye of the mountains looming in the distance.

Upon reaching the store, Izzy found Rosie waiting, leaning against the wooden post of the awning with a patient smile.

"Ana's running late, as usual," Rosie said with a teasing lilt, her eyes crinkling at the edges.

It wasn't long before Ana hurried up to them, breathless, her cheeks flushed with exertion. "Forgive me," she panted, straightening her bonnet. "William was telling me about his morning over lunch. He went into a great deal of detail about how to stitch a wound. Soon, I'll be helping him in the infirmary."

"Sounds useful," Izzy said softly.

They entered the general store together, the bell above the door announcing their arrival with a cheerful jangle. Inside, rows of fabric bolts offered a spectrum of colors and textures. Izzy liked the idea of making a dress of her own because she could wear it when the other dresses felt too fancy for an occasion.

Izzy listened intently as her sisters chatted.

"Anything here catching your eye, Izzy?" Rosie inquired, pulling her from her reverie with a gentle nudge.

"Many things," Izzy responded. When her sisters chose a fabric that came with many patterns, she chose the same fabric in a different color. At least she would feel like she was still a part of their lives if they dressed similarly.

After their purchases were made, the three sisters walked the short distance to Ana's house to spend their afternoons together.

Soon, the scent of sugar and flour mingled in the air as Izzy helped Ana roll out dough for the cookies they decided to make. As they worked, Rosie's laughter filled the room and Izzy couldn't help but think about the laughter they had shared every day of their lives. Until now. Now they lived apart, and it was still strange to Izzy.

"Isn't this just the best part? The anticipation of tasting what we've made," Ana said, her voice rich with contentment as she placed a tray into the oven.

"Yes," Izzy replied. She watched as her sisters chatted and sewed, their hands deftly threading needles and gathering fabric. They created with purpose, their every stitch an assertion of identity. As Izzy worked on her dress, she wondered how Albert would feel about her wearing it. It didn't matter though. She was sewing with her sisters, and that mattered.

"Your stitches are perfect, Izzy," Rosie commented, oblivious to the turmoil behind her sister's quiet demeanor.

"Thank you," Izzy said. But perfection in sewing felt like a paltry achievement when weighed against the silence she kept about her husband's coldness.

As the afternoon waned, Rosie glanced at the clock and sighed. "Time to head back and start supper. How quickly the day slips away."

"It really does," Izzy agreed, folding her sewing neatly. She wrapped the remaining cookies, hiding them in plain paper as if to mask the sweetness they contained.

"Shall we do this again tomorrow?" Ana asked, hopeful.

"Yes," Izzy replied, a smile playing at the corners of her mouth. "I'll come after lunch."

"Good," Ana beamed. "It's settled then."

Rosie wrapped her shawl around her shoulders and stepped outside, leaving Ana and Izzy alone for a moment. "You're always welcome here, Izzy," Ana said.

"Thank you," Izzy murmured. With a last glance at the cozy kitchen, she followed Rosie's path out the door.

Once outside, each sister went their separate way. Izzy's mind already racing ahead to a meal she would not prepare, in a house that did not yet feel like home.

As soon as she was home, Izzy joined Martha in the kitchen.

"Come now, dear, take a seat here," Martha Kirkland said, gesturing toward a sturdy oak chair at the kitchen table. She pulled out the chair, and Izzy settled into it.

Martha filled a porcelain cup with steaming tea and set it down before Izzy. "Here we are, my love," Martha offered, her hands finding comfort in the familiar motions of service. She eased into the chair opposite Izzy, her gaze soft yet piercing.

"Tell me about your journey," Martha coaxed. "The road must have been long and weary for such delicate shoulders."

Izzy's fingers curled around the cup. "It wasn't difficult," she said. "The train did all the work. The difficulty lay between my former home and the train station."

"Ah, yes," Martha murmured, a smile tugging at the corners of her lips. "A chance to plant roots, to grow strong beneath the endless sky. It must have been very difficult to marry a man you'd just met."

"It was either brave or foolish," Izzy sighed. "I scarcely know which."

"Perhaps a bit of both, but mostly courageous, I'd say." Martha reached across the table, her hand hovering just shy of Izzy's own. "You've stepped into a new world, and you must get used to life in that world. Mr. Thoreau is a good man, but he's very reserved. I don't know that I've ever really seen him display emotion in the eight years I've worked for him."

"I don't know how to talk to him. Do you have any advice for me?" Izzy asked.

"About how to talk to Mr. Thoreau? No, I haven't found the secret to that yet. You'll find your stride, and with time, I think you'll come to love it here."

"Time," Izzy said. "I wish I felt like the time would pass quickly."

"Time, and a friend," Martha added quietly, her eyes locking with Izzy's. "You've got me, child. We'll weather this season together."

Izzy nodded, the first fragile roots of trust taking hold.

Martha set the teapot aside and, with a measured motion, began to knead dough on the flour-dusted counter. Her hands worked rhythmically, as if each press and fold were a silent testament to years of unwritten stories etched deep in her palms.

"Albert's father," Martha started, "was very much like Albert, rigid in his beliefs and seeming cold to others. And Albert's mother, well, she was the water that somehow softened the stone. I watched her and learned from her. She was my dearest friend back East, and when my husband died, she wrote to Albert and told him that he should hire me." She glanced up at Izzy.

Izzy listened, her hands cupping the warmth of her tea, a small barrier between herself and the weight of expectation.

"Even the mightiest river can carve through rock," Martha continued, "not with force, but with persistence. With time." Her eyes met Izzy's. "You need to take that time to learn about Albert and let him learn about you. Albert favors hearty meals. He enjoys beef stew on Sundays, and he's partial to apple pie with a crumble top. I'll show you the recipes, the little tricks to getting the crust just so."

"Thank you," Izzy murmured. There was solace in the knowledge of these small commandments, a means to navigate the vast terrain of expectations. "Then if you want an evening off, I can cook for him."

"Patience," Martha said, dusting flour from her hands. "Patience will be your closest ally, and a pinch of sugar often sweetens more than just the pie."

Izzy clasped her hands in her lap. "Martha," she said, "I can't begin to express my gratitude for your guidance. It's...it's more than I imagined I'd find out here."

Martha looked up from her task at the basin. The corners of her mouth lifted in a smile that didn't quite chase away the shadows in her eyes.

"Child, we women have to stick together. I'll do all I can to give you guidance on being the type of wife Mr. Thoreau is needing." Her tone held the weight of unspoken stories, the kind written in the callouses of her hands and the set of her jaw.

The room filled with a comfortable silence, one that allowed Izzy's thoughts to unfurl like the quilt she'd left in her satchel, a patchwork of fear and hope stitched together.

"Did you ever regret it?" Izzy asked suddenly, her gaze catching Martha's. "Coming out here, I mean..."

"Every choice has its downside, Izzy," Martha said. "There were days I cursed the sun for rising and nights I wished the moon would forget to climb. But regrets? They're luxury. We make our choices, and we stand by them. And we find joy in everything we can."

"Joy," Izzy repeated, tasting the word as if it were new.

"Yes," Martha said. "In little things—like getting Albert's pie crust just right or seeing the first sprouts in spring. And in big things, like knowing there's someone who will stand by you, come hell or high water."

"Like you," Izzy said. "Thank you, Martha. For standing by me. I lost my mother recently, and I thought I would only have my sisters."

"Think nothing of it. Albert is a good man," Martha said, "but he's set in his ways, as men often are. You'll need patience, Izzy. Understanding, too."

Izzy met Martha's gaze, finding an unspoken kinship in the depths of her eyes. "I want to be a good wife to him, Martha. I do. But everything here is so new, so... overwhelming. I always imagined spending my days in the kitchen as my mother did. To spend a morning choosing dresses with a dressmaker is a bit of a surprise."

"Change is never easy," Martha acknowledged. "It's like breaking in a new pair of boots. At first, they pinch and rub, but given time, they form to your feet as if they were made just for you. Your marriage to Albert will be much the same. Give it time. Give yourself time."

"Is it always going to be this hard?" Izzy whispered.

"Hard?" Martha asked. "Life is difficult. But there's beauty in the struggle."

Izzy nodded, absorbing the tacit fortitude that seemed to emanate from Martha's very being. "Thank you," she murmured. "For everything you've taught me, for the kindness you've shown. I'll remember your words, Martha, and I'll try. I promise."

Martha reached across the table, her hand covering Izzy's. "You're stronger than you know, child. Remember that when the nights get cold, and the days get long."

"Strong," Izzy repeated. She almost said that the night was the only time she could be with Albert that he wasn't cold, but she knew that his housekeeper didn't need to know that about him.

"Come," Martha said, standing with a rustle of skirts. "Let's finish up here. Tomorrow's another day, and who knows what it'll bring."

Izzy wiped her hands on the apron cinched around her waist.

"Albert will be back from town soon," Martha's voice cut through Izzy's thoughts.

"Of course," Izzy replied. There were truths unspoken between them.

"Patience is a virtue hard-earned, but you'll find your way."

"Tonight," Izzy breathed to herself, "I begin anew."

She heard the front door open and hurried to remove her apron. It wouldn't please Albert to know that she'd been helping in the kitchen, so there was no reason to let him see her wearing it.

She would be the best wife to him she could possibly be. Starting now.

Chapter Five

In their bedroom, Albert and Izzy were entwined with an unexpected familiarity. Izzy marveled at how comfortable she felt with Albert when they were in bed together, but not at any other time. She wanted them to be close always, but she had a feeling that wouldn't happen.

But within the confines of their shared warmth, reality seemed to fade away. Izzy, her senses heightened, felt the world narrow down to the touch of Albert's hands, the pressure of his lips, and the steady beat of his heart against her chest.

And then, a sensation unlike any she had known before swept over her. A crescendo of pleasure that shattered the silence of the night, leaving her breathless. She clung to Albert, her voice a whisper lost in the shadows. "It's magic," she gasped, the word strange and new, yet fitting perfectly in the moment of their quiet revelation.

How could she feel such magic with a man who didn't seem to care for her during the day? It was so confusing!

The following morning, Izzy ventured out into Hope Springs. She walked slowly, deliberately, her mind still on what had transpired between her and Albert the night before.

Her fingertips grazed the delicate petals of wildflowers along the streets, much like how Albert had traced the contours of her skin.

Izzy's walk was a solitary act of reclaiming herself, step by step, from the powerlessness that marriage entailed for women. Here, she found a semblance of peace—a break from the unspoken rules and regulations that governed her life.

It was in these small moments, alone with the burgeoning day, that Izzy allowed herself to dream—dreams not of grandeur or escape, but of understanding and belonging in a place where she was more than just a mail-order bride, more than an appendage to a man of wealth and influence.

Albert Thoreau remained a mystery. There was a depth to him, hinted at in the night's embrace, that suggested more than the facade of power and control. She wished she knew the real Albert, but there was no way of knowing whether he was truly the strong, rich man who she'd married, or the tender lover, who was with her at night.

She definitely preferred the man who came out at night, but most people only saw the man he was during the day. It was hard to know.

"Mrs. Thoreau," a voice called out.

It took her a moment to realize that she was Mrs. Thoreau. She turned, her heart hitching slightly at the sight of Albert striding toward her, his presence like a boulder in the river of her thoughts—unyielding, demanding attention. Two men flanked him.

"Good day, Albert," Izzy greeted. She would love to be able to bury her face against his chest in an embrace that would never end, but instead, she was formal, as he was.

"Jonathan, Samuel, this is my wife, Isabelle," Albert introduced with a smile.

"Ma'am," they both nodded, hats briefly lifted in recognition.

"They will be dining with us on Monday night. Be sure to have Martha prepare something suitable for company," Albert said, a statement rather than an invitation as if penciling in another appointment in his ledger of ownership.

"Of course," Izzy replied, her smile practiced.

As the trio departed, Izzy turned her attention back to the street before her, eager to slip from under the weight of Albert's gaze.

The bookstore beckoned like a haven, its wooden sign creaking gently in the breeze. She stepped over the threshold, the bell above the door announcing her escape from the sun's scrutiny. The dim interior was lined with shelves, each groaning under the weight of stories and knowledge—a contrast to the stifling expectations that loomed outside.

"Can I help you find anything?" The shopkeeper, a young woman with sharp eyes, appeared from between two bookcases.

"Thank you, but I'm just browsing," Izzy responded, fingers tracing the spines of novels as she walked along the aisle.

"Ah, I see you've found our classics section," the shopkeeper commented, joining her. "Do you have a favorite author?"

"Charlotte Brontë," Izzy admitted, her touch lingering on a well-worn copy of 'Jane Eyre.' The tale of a woman's resilience against the confines of society resonated deep within her.

"An excellent choice," the woman smiled, pulling out a novel by Mary Shelley. "For me, it's 'Frankenstein.' The story of creation and the consequences that follow feels...pertinent."

They went on to discuss strong female characters and the difficulties they faced—realities not too different from their own. In the shared space between the pages of fiction, Izzy felt a kindred spirit, a subtle rebellion against the roles they were expected to fill.

"Thank you," Izzy murmured as she left the store, a new book tucked under her arm like a shield. "For the company."

"Anytime, Mrs. Thoreau," the shopkeeper said, nodding with understanding.

The town square of Hope Springs was transformed into a celebration. Albert Thoreau, with his bride Izzy at his side, eased through the throng of townsfolk gathered for the Sunday affair. The air carried the twang of banjo strings and the rhythmic clap of spoons. A man with a fiddle hurried to join the band.

"Look at this," Albert said, gesturing toward an array of tables crowned with local treats—pies, jams, and breads. Izzy's gaze lingered on the spread, her fingers grazing the edge of a table before she selected a small pastry.

"Delicious," she commented.

"Come," Albert said, guiding her past the musicians. They arrived at a space cleared for games, where the clang of metal meeting metal signified another round of horseshoes.

"Care to try your hand?" Albert asked, his voice shaded with a challenge.

"Very well," Izzy replied, accepting the heavy horseshoe. She felt its weight, a symbol of the burdens she carried silently, a reminder of the strength she mustered daily to wield her life with poise under the watchful eyes of a world that offered little room for error.

Albert explained the rules, simple yet demanding precision. Together they stood, side by side. Her first throw fell short while Albert's horseshoe arced true, encircling the stake with a triumphant clink.

"See? It's all in the wrist," he said.

Izzy nodded, her next attempt mirroring his technique. The horseshoe spun, carving through the air with defiance until it embraced the stake with a satisfying ring. A cheer erupted from the onlookers, and for a fleeting moment, Izzy tasted victory.

"Bravo, Izzy!" Albert said, his hands firm on her shoulders.

"Thank you," she said.

Together, they cheered each other on, competitors in sport but partners in the spectacle of survival.

After the game, Izzy led the way to the sanctuary of a nearby park. They chose a bench at random, sitting down together, looking out over the crowd of people there.

"Isn't it strange," Izzy said, "how we're all expected to follow paths laid out before us by others? To tread the tracks of their choosing?"

Albert, his suit no longer the armor of a businessman but the mere clothing of a man, nodded. "It's a heavy yoke, the expectations placed upon our shoulders." His eyes held a flicker of vulnerability.

"Tell me, Albert," she said, turning to face him fully, "what would you do if you weren't shackled by these...these societal chains?"

He hesitated, the question drawing a line in the sand of his carefully curated existence. "I paint," he confessed. "With oils and brushes. When I was a boy, I wanted to be an artist more than anything, but my father wanted me to go West and make my own fortune."

"Why?" Izzy asked. It wasn't that she didn't understand a parent's expectations, but it had never occurred to her that his father had pointed him to where he was now.

"Why do I paint?" he asked, deliberately misunderstanding her.

"No, why did your father not want you to paint?"

He sighed. "My father was born the eldest son of a rich man. He inherited his father's wealth. I'm the second son, and I always knew the wealth would be my brother's. Father wanted me to make my own way. He wanted to travel west himself, but my mother would never agree. So, he put the expectation on me from the time I was a small boy."

Izzy nodded. "You've never mentioned it before."

"It's not something I share," Albert admitted, his fingers tracing an absent pattern on the bench. "It's deemed...frivolous for a man to focus on the arts."

"Would you show me?" Izzy's request hung between them.

Albert looked as if he was torn by indecision. "Yes," he said. "Yes, I'll show you."

The conversation that followed would be something Izzy would look back on with a smile. He talked of what he'd once dreamed of his life to be, and she mentioned how she'd always been locked away with her sisters.

Izzy glimpsed the artist behind the entrepreneur, the dreamer within the realist. As Albert spoke of his paintings, he seemed to truly come alive before her. The same way he did in bed at night.

Albert led Izzy to his studio. It was obvious that Martha didn't know what the room was or had been told to never open the door. Or both. There were layers of dust over the cloths that covered the paintings. He pulled one cover back, unveiling a tapestry of color beneath—a silent testament to a world beyond ledgers and contracts.

Izzy's breath caught in her throat as she beheld the painting—a landscape where the wildness of nature was captured with bold strokes and impassioned hues. And in that moment, she knew her husband shouldn't have ever been a miner. What if he'd injured his hands?

"Your paintings..." Izzy whispered, "they're beautiful. I had no idea all of this was inside you!" Her husband was more than she'd seen him as. This room told her so much about him that she hadn't realized was there. She was seeing the man in a whole new light, and she was happy to know there was more to him than the boring businessman.

Albert watched her, his guarded demeanor softening. "And what of you, Isabelle? What passions lay hidden beneath your surface?"

She hesitated. Then, emboldened by their newfound kinship, Izzy divulged her own clandestine pursuit. "I write," she confessed, her voice almost a sigh. "Ridiculous little tales that make me laugh—stories of women who dare to dream within the confines of their corseted lives."

"May I...?" His inquiry trailed off, but the meaning hung clear between them.

"Perhaps, one day," she allowed. "I'm nowhere near as talented as you, and I need to get better before I show anyone."

Hand in hand, Izzy and Albert left the house and wandered to the riverbank.

"Look at the river," Izzy murmured. "So serene on the surface, yet aware of the turmoil that churns in its depths."

"Much like ourselves," Albert replied.

"Sometimes," he continued, "I wonder if we are ever truly seen for who we are, not just for the roles we're compelled to play."

"Perhaps that is why we create," Izzy mused, her eyes reflecting the twilight shimmer on the water. "To be seen, if only by the canvas or the page." She knew it was true for her. So often she'd felt invisible. Just one of a set of three. If you knew one, you knew them all.

"Your stories," Albert said at length, "they sound like liberation."

"Like your paintings," Izzy agreed.

Albert led Izzy away from the river's edge. A path, narrow and seemingly forgotten, veered into the embrace of the wild. They followed it.

At the end of the path, they found a beautiful meadow that seemed to be untouched by man. Poppies, lupines, and goldenrods painted a picture of freedom that both Izzy and Albert knew existed only within these moments.

"Look at this," Albert whispered. With careful fingers, he selected blossoms, each one a testament to the delicate balance between strength and fragility. The bouquet he fashioned for Izzy was small, but it was something she'd never expected from him. To her, it was the most precious gift she had ever received.

"Thank you," Izzy murmured. Their petals brushed against her palm. "They're beautiful!"

He produced a picnic basket from behind a rock, and she had to wonder if he'd hidden it himself or had someone else do it. He took it and spread out a blanket for them to sit on while they feasted.

There, with a simple meal shared between them, they found solace in each other's presence. The bread was coarse, the cheese sharp, every bite a reminder of life's unadorned essence.

"Sometimes I feel as trapped as these flowers must be," Izzy admitted, "rooted in place, subject to the whims of the wind."

"Yet they thrive," Albert replied, his eyes not on the flowers, but on Izzy. "Despite it all, they find a way to stand tall, to show their colors to the world."

"Is that what we're doing now?" Izzy asked. "Standing tall?"

"Perhaps," he said. "Or perhaps we're learning to bend so we don't break."

Izzy nodded. "I think that's what we're doing. Bending to fit into our lives."

He studied her for a moment but remained silent. There wasn't much to say to her if she felt that she was anywhere close to breaking.

Izzy and Albert lay back upon the worn blanket, their picnic remains tucked away in the basket. Above them, the first stars blinked into existence.

"Look there," Albert murmured, pointing toward the heavens where constellations began to reveal their ancient stories. "That cluster of stars, they call it Cassiopeia. She was a queen...condemned to the sky for her vanity."

"An eternal punishment for a woman's pride," Izzy observed. Her eyes traced the celestial pattern, finding an odd kinship in the myth—another tale of a woman bound by forces greater than herself.

"Yet, even bound, she endures," he replied. "What about you, Izzy? Beyond these open skies, what dreams do you hold?"

She turned her head to meet his gaze. "I dream of writing," she said. "To create worlds beyond this one, characters who can escape the chains that hold them." She sighed. "I dream of children and grandchildren and my sisters beside me, each with their own families. I dream of being safe from my father and him never finding us."

"Then write," Albert said. "Craft your freedom with every word." He rolled to his side to face her. "Why are you worried about your father finding you?"

"Father is...not a pleasant man. I grew up locked away from the world, and my sisters were my only companions, our mother our only teacher. She taught us a great deal, but when she died, Father...He hurt us. We left in the dead of night and ran."

"I had no idea. Do you think he's looking for you?" Albert's brows drew together.

"We really don't know. We're just happy to have found a community where we can all be near one another and still spend time together. I have never been truly alone in my life. I shared a room with my sisters. Now, I will walk around town alone, and it feels odd to me."

It was then that Albert turned to Izzy and leaned in close. His lips met hers with a tenderness that he had not shown anywhere but their bedroom. This was a kiss born not of passion but of understanding.

Izzy's response was hesitant at first, as if unsure whether to trust the emotions that surged within her. But as the kiss deepened, a warmth spread through her. When they parted, they remained embraced.

In that embrace, Izzy found hope that they would be able to continue to have a relationship apart from the bedroom.

Later, Izzy walked alongside Albert toward their home. The blanket was folded under his arm and the picnic basket was in her hand.

"Albert," she murmured, breaking the silence that had settled over them, "today... it felt like we were the only two people in the world."

He glanced at her, the corners of his mouth lifting ever so slightly in a restrained smile. "In those hours, perhaps we were," he replied.

"Next Sunday seems like a lifetime away," she confessed, pausing on the top step and turning to face him.

"Time has a way of stretching thin when we yearn for something just out of reach," Albert said.

"Today was..." Izzy struggled to find the words, her heart dancing between joy and sorrow. "It was magic, Albert. Pure magic."

"Magic is a rare thing," he responded. "We must cherish it while we can."

"I always cherish it," she said softly. Deep down, she knew they were about to go back to the way things had been. He would be warm only in the night, and she would continue to do things the way he wanted.

But she found that in their day together, her dream had changed. Now she wanted to live a full life with him and pen her stories. Before, she'd wanted to pen her stories and forget him. She wasn't sure if she was falling for him, but she had a feeling that she was. And it frightened her.

Chapter Six

Izzy stood motionless in the center of her bedroom, surrounded by an ocean of tulle and satin that cascaded from boxes the dressmaker had sent over. Each gown seemed to taunt her with silk fabrics and intricate beadwork. She lifted a hand-embroidered bodice, knowing she wouldn't feel like herself in the gown.

"Miss Izzy," Martha called from the doorway, "I'm going to start on supper if we're to be ready for your guests."

"Of course," Izzy replied as she let the fabric slip from her grasp back into the box. These dresses weren't hers; they were costumes, designed for a role she never auditioned for—a display piece to adorn Albert's world. She couldn't help but think of the man she'd spent the day with on Sunday and wonder how that man—the artist—felt about his wife wearing costumes for the world to see.

In the kitchen, the aroma of roasting meat and fresh bread filled the air, yet Izzy's mind was elsewhere, ensnared by the gowns' suffocating grandeur. She moved mechanically, chopping vegetables to help Martha with the grand dinner she was preparing. The knife's rhythmic thud against the cutting board was a stark reminder of the monotonous reality she could not escape.

"Careful there," Martha cautioned, noting the distant look in Izzy's eyes. "Wouldn't want to serve a finger with the meat."

A hollow laugh escaped Izzy's lips, her gaze flickering up to meet Martha's concerned eyes. "Seems it might be the least of my worries tonight."

"Those dresses got you all ruffled?" Martha asked, her hands deftly kneading dough.

"Ruffled and then some," Izzy admitted, setting down the knife. "They're...they're just so much, Martha. I feel like I'm drowning in someone else's dream."

"Mr. Albert expects a lot," Martha said, her tone carefully neutral, yet hinting at understanding beyond her station. "But maybe try to find a bit of yourself in the dresses. There's no harm in looking fine, even if the finery doesn't feel like it fits."

"Looking fine for him, you mean," Izzy said. "I reckon I'll always be playing dress-up for Albert's sake."

"Perhaps," Martha conceded, "but tonight, it's about more than dress-up. It's about showing them you can hold your own. You're stronger than you think, Miss Izzy."

"Strength doesn't come from silk and lace," Izzy murmured, but something in Martha's words made her determined to show everyone that she could be just what Albert wanted—a doll on the shelf for him to take down when he was ready.

"Maybe not," Martha agreed, "but sometimes, it's the armor we wear 'til we find the strength inside. Now, let's get this table set right, and show everyone what you're made of."

WITH A RELUCTANT SIGH, Izzy slipped into the deep green dress she had selected earlier. It wasn't quite as fancy as the other dresses, but she felt it suited her well. She turned before the mirror, the reflection of a woman she scarcely recognized staring back at her with hollow eyes. The door creaked open, and Albert entered the room, his expression tightening as he surveyed her appearance.

"That looks like a day dress, Isabelle," he said with a disapproving frown. Without waiting for her response, he strode over to the wardrobe and riffled through the other gowns until his fingers closed around a pale blue silk dress. Holding it up to the light, he nodded to himself. "This one. It will complement your eyes. Change into it before our guests arrive."

Izzy bit back the retort that threatened to surface and took the dress from him, her movements mechanical. When she emerged, Albert appraised her with a nod that seemed more transactional than appreciative.

"Much better," he declared.

A short while later, their guests arrived, and they sat in the dining room, the chandelier's lights all glowing over them. Izzy was glad the chandelier was rarely used because she felt as if she was on a stage beneath the lights. The dinner party unfolded under the heavy chandelier's glow, with Jonathan, Samuel, and their wives engaging in boring conversation about the weather, crops, and distant politics. There was laughter, but it felt out of place to Izzy as if there was something wrong with it. As the meal drew to a close, the men retired to the study with glasses of brandy in hand, leaving the women to gather in the drawing room.

"Your dress, Mrs. Thoreau, it's simply beautiful," commented Samuel's wife, her voice a soft trill that barely rose above the sound of the crackling fireplace.

"Thank you, Mrs. Collins," Izzy replied, smiling sweetly. She felt the weight of their gazes, the unspoken scrutiny that measured her worth in threads and seams.

"Albert has impeccable taste, does he not?" Jonathan's wife added, her words coming out as condescending.

"Yes, he does," Izzy managed to say, her hands folded neatly in her lap atop the blue silk. She wondered if they saw through the facade. One of them certainly knew that Albert had picked out her dress for her.

As the evening wore on, the women's chatter became a blurred hum to Izzy's ears. She sat there, ensconced in blue silk, feeling like a decorative piece in Albert's collection. She didn't think the other women even noticed when she stopped speaking. And when the last guest had departed and the door closed with finality behind them, Izzy stood alone in the silent house, the pale blue gown a cold comfort against the stark reality of her existence.

Izzy stood by the window, still as a statue in her pale blue silk gown. The house, once filled with the clinking of silverware and the low buzz of conversation, now echoed with emptiness.

"Isabelle," Albert's voice came from behind her, formal and controlled. She turned slowly to face him.

"Albert," she acknowledged, tucking a loose strand of hair behind her ear, a nervous habit that felt like a silent plea for mercy.

He stepped closer, the sound of his footsteps on the hardwood floor measured and deliberate. "You did well tonight," he said, his eyes scanning her face. "But we must always be conscious of how you present yourself. You are a reflection of me, of my standing in this community."

Izzy nodded, though the fabric of her dress seemed to tighten around her with each word he spoke. "I understand," she whispered.

"Good." He paused, his gaze lingering on her for a moment longer before he turned away. "There will always be occasions where you must show your best self."

WHEN HE RETURNED FROM work on Friday, Izzy rose to greet him.

"Isabelle," he said, his voice carrying the weariness of a man doing something he did not enjoy with his life. "My parents will be arriving in a month. They are eager to meet you and see my home. They live in New York, and this will be their first visit."

A cold dread settled in Izzy's stomach. His parents were wealthy, unlike her parents who had raised her and her sisters on their isolated farm. Her role as his wife would be under scrutiny, her every move watched and judged.

"Of course," she managed to say. "We will prepare accordingly."

"Yes," Albert said, the faintest trace of satisfaction in his tone. "They expect nothing less than perfection."

As he walked past her, Izzy felt the distance between them stretch out like the vast mountains surrounding Hope Springs. She knew, at that moment, that no matter how finely she dressed or how gracefully she entertained, it would always be his domain, and she was merely another asset within it.

RAIN DRUMMED RELENTLESSLY on the roof of the Thoreau mansion amid the silence between Izzy and her husband on Sunday afternoon. She watched as droplets cascaded down the windowpane. The storm had dashed Izzy's hopes of spending the afternoon outside with Albert.

Albert sat across the room in his preferred armchair. He was a fortress of a man. With a newspaper unfolded before him, his eyes scanned over the columns of ink while Izzy wondered if they could call it spending the day together if they were merely in the same room not speaking.

"Seems there's been quite the upheaval back east," Albert's voice sliced through the stillness, devoid of warmth. His thumb brushed against the paper, causing it to crackle. "It seems that the war in Cuba is finally over. It's all anyone's talking about in New York."

"Roosevelt's Rough Riders were able to take San Juan Hill," Albert continued. "It remains to be seen who will be taking control of the country, but I do hope they follow the lead of the United States and form a democracy there."

Izzy watched him, this man who had become her husband. Albert spoke of events miles away with detached authority. And yet, here in his home, even the weather dictated what freedoms Izzy could enjoy.

"I agree," Izzy murmured, knowing he wasn't looking for any real opinions from her. Her agreement was expected in the unwritten contract of their union.

Albert folded the newspaper, setting it aside with precision. "It's a man's duty to stay informed, to protect his interests," he stated. "You would do well to remember that Izzy."

Izzy concentrated on the afghan she was making—a blanket of soft blues and muted grays that would never grace her own bed. Someday, she would meet someone who needed a blanket, and she would have this one to give them. Perhaps she could crochet an entire room full of blankets for someone. Anyone.

"Who's that for?" Albert's voice cut through the room's silence.

Izzy hesitated. "It's for someone who needs it more than we do," she answered, her voice soft yet carrying the weight of her convictions.

"Charity," he said. "An admirable pursuit for a woman, I suppose."

"I would think it's an admirable pursuit for anyone. Helping others is something Jesus talked about often."

"See that it doesn't interfere with your duties," Albert said simply.

"Of course," Izzy replied, her tone carefully neutral. She wanted to please him, but he didn't seem to be happy with anything she did. How she wished she could see the man who had lain beneath the stars with her the previous week.

ON MONDAY AFTERNOON, she met up with her sisters at Ana's house as she did most weekday afternoons.

"Rosie, Ana," Izzy said. "Albert's parents will be here next month."

Her sisters exchanged glances, the kind filled with silent words and unspoken understandings. Anabelle, ever the firebrand, was quick to respond.

"His parents? Are you nervous?" Ana asked.

"Petrified actually." Izzy sighed. "And I fear it'll mean endless days of dressing up like some porcelain doll on display."

"Surely it won't be that bad, Izzy," Rosabelle interjected. "You've managed everything else thrown your way thus far."

"Managed?" Izzy shook her head. "I feel more akin to a puppet, Rosie. Every move orchestrated, every smile rehearsed. And now with them coming..." She hadn't told her sisters how she felt in her marriage, and she knew now was the time.

Rosie took Izzy's hand. "You've talked about how lovely it is in bed with him. Certainly, he loves and appreciates you."

Izzy laughed softly, but the sound wasn't one of amusement. "That's the only time he's truly himself. Well, and one lovely Sunday afternoon that feels as though it never happened."

"Perhaps it's just for show," Ana suggested.

"Show," Izzy echoed hollowly. "That's all we are to them, aren't we? Props in a grand play of wealth and power."

Ana shook her head. "That's not how my marriage is. William has me help him in the infirmary, and he tells me I'm doing a wonderful job quite often. I feel that we have a good marriage, though I do wish he'd tell me he loves me."

Izzy set her tea down and frowned. "It's not like that with us. Albert is always concerned about my appearance and tells me how I'm representing him."

"Let's not borrow trouble from tomorrow," Rosie said softly. "We'll face this together, as we always have."

"But you won't be there with his parents all the time. I will," Izzy said, wishing her sisters would be there. Their presence made everything easier for her.

WHEN ALBERT ARRIVED home that afternoon, he mentioned his plans for his parents' visit. "We'll be hosting a grand party in honor of my parents' visit," he stated. "It will be an opportunity for them to see the life we've built here."

Izzy's fingers clenched tightly around the fabric of her skirt, the rough texture grounding her.

"Your sisters are to attend as well," he continued, his gaze lingering on her with an intensity that felt like scrutiny. "They must present themselves fittingly. I shall arrange for dresses to be made for each of them. Our family's image must remain impeccable."

Izzy wanted to scream at him that he could control her, but her sisters weren't his to dress and command. "I'll ask them if they'd mind attending and wearing the dresses you prefer."

"You'll need to convince them if they are unwilling," he said shortly.

"I'll do my best," she said.

THE NEXT DAY, SEATED at Ana's worn kitchen table with her sisters, Izzy relayed the news. "Albert insists you both need new dresses for the party," she said. "He's going to have the modiste that made my dresses make them for you."

"New dresses?" Rosie's brow creased with concern, but there was resignation in her posture, a silent acceptance of the role they were all forced to play.

"Does he think us dolls to be dressed up for his amusement?" Ana's voice crackled with frustration. "I'm sorry, Izzy. I shouldn't have said that. You have to live with his control every day, and I have to do it once, and I'm complaining."

"Don't worry about it," Izzy replied. "I hate it as well, but we've little choice in the matter."

"Then we'll wear the dresses," Rosie declared after a moment. "For your sake, Izzy. We stand together, always."

Ana nodded in agreement, though her lips were a tight line, betraying her inner turmoil. "Of course we will. We love you, Izzy!"

As the conversation turned to lighter matters, Izzy's mind wandered to the party. She imagined the opulence, the laughter that would ring hollow in her ears. Yet beneath the dread, a spark of resolve took hold. For now, she would don the silk and smile through the charade.

THE MODISTE'S PARLOR was a small, suffocating room embroidered with the incessant hum of the sewing machine. Heavy drapes trapped the light and the air, lacing the atmosphere with the musty scent of fabric and mothballs. Izzy stood on an ornate pedestal. Her sisters flanked her, forms draped in unfinished silk and taffeta.

She was happy they were no longer forced to always dress alike, but at that moment, the idea of presenting a united front with her triplets seemed to be the only answer. Together, they could dress alike, and maybe she could blend in with the sisters she loved so dearly.

"Keep still," the modiste chided gently as she pinned the hem of the pale blue gown, her fingers deft.

"Does it have to be so tight?" Rosie murmured, her voice muffled behind the pins held between her lips.

"Beauty knows discomfort," the modiste replied. "And these gowns must speak volumes."

Ana shifted restlessly, the rustle of her skirts a soft rebellion against the silence. "They'll talk our ears off at this rate."

Izzy caught Ana's eye in the mirror, and she felt a giggle bubbling up inside her. Oh, how she loved her sister and the sarcasm that seemed to drip from her lips when they were together.

Later, seated around the kitchen table cluttered with recipe books and scribbled notes, the Winslow sisters and Martha plotted the menus as generals might plan a siege.

It was the first time Izzy's sisters had been invited into her home, and she was embarrassed of the wealth dripping from every room.

"Albert's parents have sophisticated palates," Martha began. "We must impress without seeming to try too hard."

"Roast duck, then," Ana suggested. "A dish to dazzle yet not overshadow."

"Followed by a delicate lemon tart," Rosie added, the practicality in her voice doing little to mask the strain beneath. "Simple elegance."

"Two weeks of performances," Izzy mused aloud. "Can we sustain the masquerade that long?"

Martha placed a comforting hand atop Izzy's. "We will manage, dear. And it's more Albert's father who we must worry about. His mother and I grew up running around the streets of New York together like homeless urchins."

Their conversation continued, each dish debated and decided upon, but Izzy's thoughts strayed to the dresses that lay upstairs, symbols of a life constrained by a corset. The feast they planned was nothing more than another charade they must perform.

"Every supper will be a spectacle," Izzy said quietly as they finalized the last dessert. "Every bite a reminder that I must be perfect at all times."

IZZY STOOD BEFORE THE gleaming kitchen table, her fingers tracing the grain of the wood as if seeking wisdom from its polished surface. Arrayed before her were china and silver, crystal and linen.

"Remember now, elbows off the table and speak only when spoken to," Martha advised, her words clipped yet not unkind. "His father believes in the old ways. A wife must know her place."

"Of course," Izzy murmured. The weight of expectation bore down on her shoulders.

"Compliment his mother on her attire; it's a safe topic," Martha continued. "And always defer to the father, his word is law in their eyes."

"Law…" Izzy wanted to vomit. His father sounded much like her own father, and she and her sisters were not ones to deal with criticism lightly.

"Never raise your voice, nor offer opinions too freely. They see it as impertinence. You represent Albert now. Your words, your very breath, carry his reputation."

"His reputation," Izzy repeated, the phrase catching in her throat like a thorn. Every syllable was a reminder of her confinement within invisible walls.

"Is there more?" Izzy asked.

"Only this," Martha said, laying a hand on Izzy's arm—a fleeting connection that spoke of shared burdens. "Smile, even if it pains you. In his father's world, everyone at least pretends to be happy."

"Smile," Izzy consented. A smile that didn't quite reach her eyes, a mask worn so often it threatened to become her face.

"Good," Martha approved with a nod, her expression softening ever so slightly. "Now, let's go over the dinner conversation once more."

With each instruction, Izzy felt herself receding, her identity dissolving into the role she was compelled to inhabit. She was learning more than just the art of conversation; she was learning the cost of survival in a world that demanded her silence.

Chapter Seven

Albert's father stepped down onto the street in front of Izzy and Albert's home, his posture as rigid as the high collar of his shirt. With an air of authority, he surveyed the property with a critical eye. His mother followed suit, descending from the carriage with grace, her expression neutral.

Izzy watched from the porch, the fabric of the dress she wore scratching against her skin like a relentless reminder of her place in this arrangement. She clasped her hands in front of her, the chiffon sleeves too tight around her arms, as if they were trying to squeeze out the last drops of her independence.

Albert approached his parents, his gait mimicking the stiff propriety of his father's. "Father, Mother, may I introduce you to Mrs. Isabelle Thoreau," he said.

"Mrs. Thoreau," his father acknowledged with a curt nod, his gaze appraising her as though she were a possession rather than a bride.

"Mrs. Thoreau," echoed his mother in a tone that was devoid of emotion. Her eyes, a mirrored version of Albert's unforgiving gray, scrutinized Izzy as if searching for flaws.

"Mr. Thoreau, Mrs. Thoreau," Izzy replied, her throat tight as she forced the words past the lump of anxiety. She offered a tentative smile, one which neither parent felt compelled to return.

"Your attire is quite...elaborate for the afternoon," Mrs. Thoreau commented.

"Thank you, ma'am," Izzy managed to say, her cheeks burning with the knowledge that Albert had insisted on her wearing the ostentatious gown. "Albert chose it for me."

"Come inside," Albert interjected, steering the conversation away from Izzy's discomfort. "We have much to discuss."

As the family moved into the house, Izzy trailed behind. Her two weeks of torture was just beginning.

Albert guided his father toward his private sanctuary. As the study door clicked shut, a silence descended upon the foyer.

"Mrs. Thoreau," Izzy began, "would you care for some tea?"

"Lead the way, my dear," Mrs. Thoreau replied, her voice suddenly excited and enthusiastic.

Martha greeted Mrs. Thoreau with unexpected tenderness, wrapping her in an embrace that seemed to dissolve the formidable façade she shared with her son.

"Martha, you remember Mrs. Thoreau?" Izzy said as though introducing strangers, yet the women's laughter mingled like that of old friends reunited.

"Of course, child. Sit, sit," Martha insisted, guiding them to the table where steam rose from a porcelain teapot and cookies lay temptingly on a plate.

As they settled into the chairs, Izzy felt a strange sense of camaraderie. The china clinked against saucers, and golden crumbs fell like confetti.

"Albert tells me you've seen his paintings," Mrs. Thoreau remarked.

Izzy hesitated, caught off guard. "Yes, once. They're...quite good," she answered, her confusion seeping through. Albert had unveiled his artistry but once.

"Ah, my husband never did approve," Mrs. Thoreau sighed, the weight of her words pressing down upon the room. "He thought it a frivolous pursuit for a man of business. But our son has been caged by the world for too long. If painting frees him, who are we to bar the door?"

Izzy listened, the revelation surprising her. The image of Albert, brush in hand, lost in the hues of his creation—was it a vision of the man he could have been? The man he still might become, if not for the chains of legacy and duty that bound him?

"Is that so?" Izzy murmured, her heart aching with newfound understanding. Mrs. Thoreau nodded, her eyes reflecting a sorrow that knew the pain of dreams deferred and spirits broken.

In that kitchen, a bond was forged. Izzy glimpsed the humanity within Mrs. Thoreau, a kindred spirit cloaked in the trappings of high society—a woman, much like herself. She'd expected his mother to be as cold as Albert could be, but it simply wasn't the case.

Izzy shifted in her seat. She met Mrs. Thoreau's gaze, a silent understanding passing between them. The air was thick with the scent of steeping tea and the sweet tang of citrus from the cookies.

"I...I agree with you," Izzy ventured, her words tentative yet earnest. "Art shouldn't be stifled. Albert's work, it's quite remarkable."

Mrs. Thoreau's lips curved into a wistful smile, a mere whisper of rebellion. "Yes. But my husband has his notions of what is proper for men of our standing. For Albert."

"Surely," Izzy pressed, hands clasped around her cup as if to draw strength from its warmth, "you don't always share those notions?"

A calculated gleam flickered in Mrs. Thoreau's eyes, the blue depths holding untold stories of battles waged in silence. "My dear," she began, voice low and conspiratorial, "the art of marriage, especially in our circles, is much like a public performance. One must always appear in agreement with one's spouse."

"Even if you disagree?" Izzy's voice cracked.

"Especially then." Mrs. Thoreau leaned closer, and their shared breath mingled in the space between them. "In public, unity is paramount. But in private," she glanced toward the door, "in private, a wife may speak her mind."

Izzy wondered if it would work for her and Albert. She hoped that she, like Mrs. Thoreau, could learn to keep her husband happy, but not lose herself.

"Thank you," Izzy murmured.

"Remember, my dear," Mrs. Thoreau said as she stood, "strength can be found even within the confines of our roles. We just have to know where to look for it."

Izzy led Mrs. Thoreau through a narrow corridor, the floorboards creaking underfoot, betraying their passage to the studio where Albert's secrets lay in colors and strokes on canvas.

"Albert rarely lets anyone in here," she confessed, as if the very walls were listening.

Mrs. Thoreau's gaze swept the room, lingering on the half-finished canvases, the riot of colors that spoke of a spirit longing to soar beyond the confines of societal dictates. "It's...quite something," she said, her words hanging heavy with unspoken thoughts.

"Writing has always been my refuge," Izzy found herself admitting. "In stories, I could weave realities where women need not bend."

"Would you show me some of your work?" Mrs. Thoreau asked, her eyes brightening with interest.

A cold draft whispered through the room, and Izzy wrapped her arms around herself. "My writings are but trifles," she demurred, the familiar cloak of modesty settling upon her shoulders. "Not worthy of attention."

"Trifles, perhaps," Mrs. Thoreau mused, stepping closer to peer at a painting where light battled shadow on the canvas, "but even trifles can hold power when they're born of truth."

The silence hung between them, a tapestry of unvoiced dreams and stifled creativity. Izzy's fingers brushed against the coarse grain of the wooden table, tracing patterns that mirrored the swirling chaos in her heart. She wished she could share her words with Mrs. Thoreau, but fear clamped down on her tongue like a vice. Her writing was a sanctuary, too sacred and vulnerable to be exposed another's gaze.

"Two nights from now," Mrs. Thoreau began, "we'll have that party. Albert insists it's essential for his business relations."

"Ah, yes, the party," Izzy said. She imagined the sea of faces, all expecting her to play the part of the doting wife. The thought sent a shiver down her spine.

"Are you looking forward to it?" Mrs. Thoreau inquired, a subtle tilt to her head suggesting she already knew the answer.

Izzy hesitated, then shook her head slightly. "My sisters and I used to dream about grand balls and social gatherings back home," she confessed, the memories bittersweet on her lips. "But now..."

"Your sisters?" Mrs. Thoreau prodded gently, coaxing the words from Izzy's reluctant heart.

"Triplets," Izzy said, a faint smile tugging at the corners of her mouth as she pictured Ana's fiery mane, Rosie's calm gaze, and her own reflection sandwiched between them. "We were inseparable. Each with our own strengths, and our own burdens."

"Sounds like a formidable trio," Mrs. Thoreau remarked.

"Indeed, we were." Izzy's smile faded, sorrow seeping into her tone. "Our mother...she passed, leaving us to fend for ourselves. I miss her guidance, her laughter."

A heavy sigh escaped Mrs. Thoreau, aged lines deepening around her eyes. "To lose one's mother is to wander adrift on an unforgiving sea," she murmured, reaching out to place a comforting hand atop Izzy's.

"Sometimes I feel I'm still searching for the shore," Izzy whispered.

"Perhaps together, we can find it," Mrs. Thoreau offered.

"Thank you," Izzy managed, wishing she trusted that such a thing could happen. "I would cherish that."

They sat in shared silence, united by a kinship born of loss and longing, their spirits tethered by invisible threads that defied the constraints of their gilded cages.

AT SUPPER THAT NIGHT, Izzy nibbled at her meal, the food rich and heavy on her tongue, though her appetite had been whittled down by the day's emotional tumult.

Across from her, Mrs. Thoreau's face was softened in the candlelight, the harsh lines of society's expectations smoothed away by their earlier confidences. The woman who had entered their home with a frosty air now exuded a warmth that drew Izzy toward her as surely as a moth to flame.

"This meal is divine, my dear," Mrs. Thoreau murmured, a smile gracing her lips as she dabbed them delicately with a napkin.

"Thank you," Izzy replied. "Martha has been an absolute treasure."

As the men excused themselves from the table, Albert led his father to the study with a stiff-backed resolve that mirrored his father's rigid posture. The door closed with a soft but definitive click.

Left in the wake of their absence, Izzy turned to Mrs. Thoreau, the silence left by the men thickening the air between them. "Would you—might you care to join me tomorrow afternoon?" Izzy ventured. "I would dearly love for you to meet my sisters in a more casual situation than the party."

"Your sisters?" Mrs. Thoreau inquired. "Do they live nearby?"

"Yes, we..." Izzy hesitated, "We have plans to spend the afternoon together. They are...lively, full of stories and laughter. I think—I hope—you might enjoy their company."

A glimmer of excitement flickered in Mrs. Thoreau's eyes. "I would be honored, Isabelle," she said.

"Then it's settled," Izzy said, a tentative smile breaking through her reserve. In that simple exchange, a bond was forged, not of duty or obligation, but of mutual respect.

IZZY LED MRS. THOREAU down the path to her sister's home.

At her sister's abode, the door swung open to reveal a room alive with the clatter of needles. Her sisters, reflections of spirited defiance, greeted Mrs. Thoreau with an eagerness that bordered on audacity. Yet, beneath the laughter and chatter, there was the special closeness that comes with being a triplet.

"Mrs. Thoreau," one sister said, holding out a half-finished blanket, the colors vibrant against the drab backdrop of the room, "today we're working on making blankets for the poor."

"Please, call me Eleanor," Mrs. Thoreau corrected gently, accepting the fabric and letting her fingers trace the patterns. "This is beautiful work."

"I do so wish Albert would do more with his painting. He's made enough money to see you comfortably for years. He should work on his art."

"I wish I could convince him to do so," Izzy said, shaking her head. "He fears his father's disapproval."

"Ah," Eleanor nodded slowly. "We need to encourage him. I think we could tell him what he does is wonderful a thousand times, and he would only hear his father's criticism."

At the end of the afternoon, when it was time to leave, Eleanor looked at Ana. "Thank you for allowing me to join you today," she said. "Today, I have been reminded of the strength that lies within us all, even when the voices that would diminish it seem deafening."

Chapter Eight

Shortly before the party was set to begin, Izzy smiled as her sisters came to the door. When they'd had their dresses made for the party, they'd had them all made in the exact same style, but different colors. Ana's gown shimmered green, Rosie's was sky blue, and Izzy was enveloped in red.

"I worry Albert will be upset that we're dressed alike," Izzy murmured. It had seemed like a good idea when they'd all inadvertently chosen the same style, but as they got closer to the party, Izzy worried they'd made a mistake.

"Let Albert tend to his businesses and leave the dresses to us," Ana said with a dismissive wave of her hand. Her own husband was a great deal more laid back than Albert.

"Yes," Rosie chimed in, her smile bright. "We are triplets. He should be happy we're not all wearing the same color."

Izzy's lips twitched into a brief smile, but it was fleeting, chased away by the weight of her duty as Albert's wife and hostess of the evening's affair. They entered the house, their gowns whispering secrets with every step.

Izzy had hired several women from town to act as maids for the party, and they all scurried about, arranging silverware with meticulous care and aligning chairs with geometric precision. Five women from town, their hands quick and nimble, were draped in plain aprons that belied the magnitude of the task ahead. It was a dinner party followed by dancing.

"Ensure the crystal sparkles," Izzy instructed one of the maids, her voice steady though her heart thundered a wild rhythm. "And the linens must be free of any creases."

"Of course, Mrs. Thoreau," the maid replied, her eyes briefly meeting Izzy's before flitting away.

"Everything will be perfect, Izzy," Ana said, her voice soothing.

"Perfection is a costly endeavor," Izzy replied. The gravity of her role, the need for approval from her husband and society, weighed upon her like the heavy lace train of her gown.

"Then let us bear the cost together," Rosie added, her hand finding Izzy's.

Izzy felt the weight of Albert's disapproval from across the dining room. She felt the color drain from her cheeks despite the bold hue of her gown. The identical dresses her sisters wore seemed to amplify her discomfort.

"Albert," came the stern yet tender intervention of Mrs. Thoreau, her hand resting on her son's arm with authority. She guided him away from the gathering, her words whispered but laced with conviction. "The girls have always been as one, since birth. Izzy told me that they were always dressed identically before coming here."

"Mother, this is not a children's birthday celebration. This is my home," Albert retorted.

"Perhaps, but tonight they wanted to celebrate their unity, their bond. They don't ordinarily indulge such whims. Allow them this symbol of sisterhood," she urged, her eyes softening at the edges with empathy—for both her son and the young woman he'd married.

"Unity..." Albert said, the word leaving a bitter taste. He glanced back at Izzy. She did look fetching in the dress.

The front door announced new arrivals with its grandiose creak, redirecting attention from the familial tete-a-tete. In strode William and Charles, both in tailored suits. Albert was happy to see his friends.

"Albert, I trust you've heard about Thompson?" Charles's voice boomed, a gregarious sound that filled the room. His eyes held a glint of triumph.

"Yes I have," Albert replied. "Caught like a rat in a trap, I hear."

"More like a snake in a henhouse," William chimed in, his doctor's hands folded neatly behind his back. "But Hope Springs can breathe easier now, knowing the viper has been defanged."

"Justice in our time," Charles declared. "The town will recover. And your mines will stop being sabotaged."

The wooden floor creaked beneath Izzy's hesitant steps as she was led into the dance by Albert, his hand firm on her waist. The musicians drew their bows across violin strings in a melody that sang of tradition and grace—a language foreign to Izzy's ears and feet. Around them, couples glided in practiced harmony, a sea of swirling gowns and tailored suits.

"Albert," she began, "I'm sorry, I..."

"Isabelle," he interrupted with a sigh, "you are stepping on my foot again."

"I never learned to waltz," she admitted, cheeks flushed with embarrassment.

"Never learned?" Albert asked, his tone sharpening with incredulity. "Your upbringing continues to perplex me. What kind of life forbids a girl from dancing?"

"Mine did," she said simply. The heat of shame crawled up her neck, branding her with the stigma of her past.

They moved awkwardly, disjointedly, until the song mercifully ended. Albert offered a curt nod before excusing himself, leaving Izzy standing alone.

"May I have this dance, Isabelle?"

She turned to find Clyde, Albert's father, extending his hand—a lifeline in a stormy sea. With a grateful smile, she took it, and together they joined the other dancers. Clyde led with a gentle patience that coaxed her through the steps without judgment or condescension.

"My wife tells me you girls always dressed alike...like triplets," Clyde said.

"Yes, until we moved here, our only clothes were identical. We are triplets, you see," Izzy replied, finding unexpected strength in the admission.

"You remind me so much of Eleanor when she was your age," Clyde continued a nostalgic gleam in his eye. "Her spirit, her fire—it seems to live on in you."

Izzy blinked, taken aback by the comparison to the wife he loved. In that moment, Izzy felt a flicker of kinship with Eleanor—another soul who had perhaps danced along the precipice of expectations and propriety.

"Thank you, Mr. Thoreau," she whispered, allowing herself to be twirled elegantly under Clyde's guiding hand.

"Please," he chuckled softly, "call me Clyde."

As the music swelled around them, Izzy allowed the rhythm to carry her away from the difficulties of the evening. In the arms of Albert's father, she found a brief respite from the scrutiny that seemed to lay claim to every other facet of her new life.

Izzy flitted between the clusters of guests. Her eyes searched for any sign of disharmony, any glass left unfilled or a smile that didn't quite reach the eyes, any detail that could betray the veneer of perfection she strove to uphold. Amidst the laughter and clinking silverware, Izzy's heart was heavy, burdened by Albert's stern admonitions.

"Rosie, dear, make sure the Hendersons have everything they need," Izzy whispered to her sister. Rosie nodded, her sky-blue gown catching the light as she moved with youthful grace toward the elderly couple. Ana, garbed in green, approached Izzy with a furrowed brow.

"Are you well?" Ana asked.

"Yes, of course," Izzy replied, forcing a smile that felt more like a grimace. "Just ensure the music continues without pause."

Ana placed a reassuring hand on Izzy's arm before she glided back into the throng, leaving Izzy to her silent vigil.

Finally, as the last guest departed with a flourish of thanks, Izzy breathed a sigh of relief. The door closed with a definitive thud, sealing away the outside world. Albert turned to his parents, the grand patriarch, and matriarch who had observed the night's events with quiet pride.

"Mother, Father, thank you for your support this evening," Albert said.

"Goodnight, my dear," Albert's mother replied.

"Son," Clyde added with a nod toward Albert, before turning to Izzy. "You did well tonight, Izzy."

"Goodnight, Clyde," Izzy replied. She watched as Albert's parents retreated to their quarters, her gaze lingering on their retreating forms.

"Goodnight," she said again.

The party had been a success, but it was a victory hard-won and hollow, for no amount of planning or poise could shield her from the cold draft of disapproval that seemed to seep from Albert's very being.

The door to their room closed with a hushed click, its finality sealing them away from the remnants of revelry that had cascaded through the house. She stood motionless.

"Albert," she said. "This evening, I felt your displeasure more keenly than ever before." Her hands wrung at the fabric of her red gown, the one that marked her as distinct yet inseparably tied to her sisters.

"Is this about the dresses?" Albert asked.

"Partly," she admitted, lifting her head to meet his eyes. "You see us adorned in finery, standing out like exotic birds amongst the drab, but what you don't grasp is that this...us wearing the same style—it's a part of who we are. We may wear different colors now, but once, we shared even that."

"And the dancing," Izzy continued. "I've never learned how to dance. My childhood was a locked room, not a ballroom, Albert. I couldn't have learned, even if I'd wanted to."

"Isabelle," he said, and she noted the use of her full name, formal and distancing. Yet, when he spoke again, his tone was softer. "I failed to consider your circumstances. It was unfair of me." His hand, hesitant, reached out to touch her arm. "Forgive me."

The word 'forgive' echoed in her mind, unfamiliar and unexpected. For a moment, Izzy allowed herself to believe that perhaps there was room for understanding.

"Truly?" It was hard to believe he even knew how to be sorry for his bad behavior.

Albert's eyes flickered with an unfamiliar warmth. "Truly," he affirmed, and there was no mistaking the sincerity that laced his voice.

In that singular moment, Izzy felt the axis of their world tilt, ever so slightly, granting her a glimpse of something she had never dared to imagine. Power. Not the kind wielded with fists or born of wealth, but the subtle, intoxicating power of being heard...of being seen.

"Then I—" She hesitated, her next words teetering on the precipice of this newfound landscape. "I accept your apology, Albert."

As they came together, the touch of his lips against hers was soft, a question rather than a claim. With each delicate caress, with every careful exploration, Izzy surrendered to the sensation of being cherished. Albert's arms encircled her, drawing her into the shelter of his embrace—a fortress built not of stone and mortar, but of flesh and bone and beating hearts.

Later, as they lay entwined beneath the weight of quilts and the quiet aftermath of connection, Albert held her close.

For the first time since she'd stepped off the train, Izzy felt a profound sense of belonging. Here, in the stillness of the night, with Albert's arms wrapped around her, she was no longer just a mail-order bride fulfilling her role. She was Isabelle Thoreau, a woman with a name, a will, and a place in the heart of a man who had finally listened.

Chapter Nine

It was with a sense of great loss that Izzy said goodbye to Albert's parents as they returned home to New York City. She was surprised at how close she felt to both of them after their visit.

She hadn't expected to like his father at all, but she'd found him warm and kind. As they drove off, she had tears in her eyes, and she told Albert she wished they could stay longer, though she was surprised.

He'd put his arm around her and pulled her to him. "We'll see them again. Perhaps next time, we can take the train to New York City."

She smiled. "I'd like that a lot. I've never been anywhere but the little house we lived in and here."

He shook his head. "I wish I could understand why your father kept you and your sisters under such careful control."

"I don't even care why," she said softly. "The man was cruel, and I never even want to think about him." She said the words with more passion than she'd shown in their months together, and he looked at her with surprise. She seemed to truly despise her father.

He hoped that she understood all men weren't like him.

IZZY AWOKE WITH A START, her stomach churning like a tempestuous sea. She clutched the edge of the bed, steadying herself against the waves of nausea that threatened to sweep her away. For several days now, sickness had greeted her at dawn, an unwelcome visitor persisting with cruel punctuality.

She rose and made her way to the washbasin. Splashing her face with water did little to ease the queasiness that knotted her insides. There was no more denying it. She needed answers, and the only place she could seek them was at the infirmary.

Dr. William Mercer, her brother-in-law, was already tending to a miner with a bandaged head by the time Izzy arrived. Dr. Mercer excused himself from his patient with a nod, his brow furrowed in concern as he caught sight of Izzy's pallor.

After Izzy described her symptoms to William, he told her, "You're expecting."

The words were meant to be joyous, but they landed like stones in Izzy's stomach. A baby. Her mind raced with the implications, the weight of responsibility, the fear of the unknown. Most of all, there was Albert, her husband, whose world seemed so distant from the one she inhabited.

She left the infirmary with her secret cradled close to her heart, the knowledge of life growing inside her made her both hopeful and frightened. As she walked through the quiet streets, the town of Hope Springs carried on unaware, its residents caught in the throes of their daily struggles for survival within the confines of a world that demanded resilience.

Back at home, she watched Albert from across the room. She only felt close to him at night, in the privacy of their bedroom. Would he welcome the child as a blessing or see it as a burden? Could she carve out a place for herself in his life that was more than just a convenient arrangement?

For now, she held her silence, allowing the truth to simmer within her as she contemplated the future. The decision to wait was hers alone. It felt good to be in control of something, and when she told him she was pregnant was something she could easily control.

THE NEEDLE DIPPED AND rose, swift as the swallows that skirted the eaves of Ana's home. Izzy's fingers worked with a quiet urgency, stitching tiny garments for an infant that fate had deposited on Ana's doorstep like a parcel with no return address. Lillian, they had named her, a moniker plucked from the air as though it had always been destined for the child with no history.

"Every baby deserves a fresh start," Ana had murmured. They sat side by side, the rhythm of their sewing a silent pact against the chaos that brewed beyond these walls. "We have asked and can't find where she came from, so we're going to keep her. After seeing so many childbirths, I don't want children of my own."

Yet, as the sisters created, Albert dismantled. The clink of coin and scratch of quill on paper echoed through his study, each signature severing ties to the empire he'd built. His ledger lay open, its columns a testament to an existence measured in profits and losses. But the numbers held no sway over him now. They were just figures numbers. He'd proven to his father that he could be a successful businessman, and now he was ready to go on with his life as he wanted.

"Albert, are you certain about this?" Charles asked, looking concerned.

"Certainty is a luxury of the naive," Albert replied, not looking up from the document he was signing. "I've seen myself through my father's eyes—a businessman without a cause. A puppet dancing on inherited strings."

"But your businesses—they're your life's work."

"Work that holds no meaning," Albert said. "Let them go. I'm tired of living to please someone else."

No one seemed to understand Albert's need to sell the businesses and live life the way he wanted to live, but he had a feeling Izzy would understand. He couldn't think of anyone's opinion who would matter more to him.

"ALBERT IS SELLING ALL his businesses." Izzy told her sisters as they sewed with Lillian in her cradle.

"Will he be all right?" Ana asked.

"I think so," Izzy responded, her thoughts straying to the baby she carried. "Or perhaps we are all just pieces on a board, moved by hands we cannot see." She shook her head. "Sometimes I feel like I'm a character in a novel, and the writer spends all his time thinking about ways to torment me."

Rosie laughed. "You know that can't be true. Or he'd be controlling all of us, and everything we think and do."

"He is a crazy man, isn't he?" Ana asked, laughing with Rosie.

Izzy just continued to stitch a gown for the baby. But she wasn't as certain as her sisters that her theories were wrong.

THE CANVAS STRETCHED across the wooden frame, as blank and barren as Albert's future seemed to him. Izzy watched her husband from the doorway of their parlor, now repurposed into an impromptu studio with a makeshift easel standing at the center.

"Albert," she began, her voice steady but soft, carrying the weight of her concern. "You've let your talents go dormant, buried under ledgers and deeds that strangle your soul."

He did not turn to face her, his gaze fixed on the emptiness before him. A sigh shuddered through his frame, betraying the turmoil within.

"Businesses...they are just things," she continued, stepping forward. "But painting, it's who you are. It's your breath, your blood. Your mother made a point of asking me to encourage your art while she was here. She hates that you gave it up to please your father."

His chuckle was a hollow sound, more bitter than amused. "What is a legacy to a man who feels he has lost his grip on the world?"

"Your art could be your rebellion—your declaration of freedom," Izzy insisted, closing the space between them. Her hand reached out, fingers brushing the coarse fabric of the unused canvas. "Create something beautiful, something from inside you. Don't worry if anyone will ever see it or love it. It's for you, not for them!"

Albert turned slowly, his eyes meeting hers. He thought back to the time when the sun coming up had been something he'd wanted to paint. Now it was simply something that told him it was time to get out of bed and start his day. He needed to get back to the man who wanted to paint.

"Perhaps," he murmured. He was glad she was encouraging him and not upset that he was changing his entire life.

Time passed—the days stretching into weeks—and the parlor began to fill with the scent of oil paints and turpentine. Albert's hands, once idle except for the signing away of his empire, moved with purpose across the canvas. Strokes of color bled life into the fibers, each hue a testament to a passion rekindled.

Izzy found herself watching less and participating more, handing him brushes, and mixing colors. Each day, Albert spent more time before his easel, the businessman fading as the artist took form.

As the paintings multiplied, leaning against the walls of the parlor-turned-studio so did a sense of peace that neither had known before. In the quiet moments, they found they genuinely liked each other and the people they were becoming.

"Thank you," he said one evening.

"For what?" Izzy asked, although she knew.

"For seeing me," Albert replied.

Every day as they grew closer, Izzy thought about telling him of the child she carried, but she still didn't know how he felt about her, and she needed to know that he cared for Izzy and not just the mother of his unborn child.

IZZY HESITATED AT THE threshold of the parlor, her fingers lightly brushing against the frame of a painting that caught the soft, morning light. It depicted a lone tree atop a knoll against the tempestuous sky above it. For some reason it spoke to Izzy in a way that few other paintings did.

"Albert," she began, her voice carrying a quiet strength that belied the unease churning within her, "might I give this one to Rosie?"

He paused his back to her, a silent figure amidst the chaos of paints and paint-smeared rags. Finally, he turned, his eyes tracing the lines of the painting as if seeing it for the first time. "Yes," he consented.

"Thank you." Izzy's gratitude was genuine but heavy with the weight of unspoken fears for her sister.

Later, as Izzy held the wrapped canvas in her arms, she found Rosie sitting alone on the porch of the house she shared with Charles. The boards creaked underfoot, announcing Izzy's presence before words could.

"Rosie," Izzy said softly, extending the package toward her sister.

Rosie looked up, her smile a practiced curve that didn't quite reach her eyes. She accepted the gift, fingers trembling as they tore through the paper to reveal the image beneath. For a moment, there was only stillness, the kind that comes before the storm.

Then, as if the dam of her composure had been breached by the sight of the solitary tree standing strong against the darkening heavens, Rosie's smile faltered, gave way to tears that streaked down her cheeks like rain on window glass.

"Isabelle…" Her voice cracked, and she clutched the painting to her chest as though it were a lifeline. "It's…it's like he saw right into my soul."

Izzy reached out, her hand resting on Rosie's shoulder with a gentle firmness. "You're not alone in this, Rosie," she murmured.

THE AUTUMN AIR HELD a chill as Izzy made her way to Ana's house. Rosie walked beside her. They moved with purpose, their breaths visible in the cold.

Once inside Ana's warm, modest home, they found little Lillian Mercer, swaddled and nestled in a handmade cradle that creaked gently with the rhythm of her slumbering breaths. Izzy's fingers grazed the infant's cheek, marveling at the innocence of the baby.

"I hope she grows up with more freedom than we had," Izzy whispered, more to herself than to Rosie, as they set about their tasks—warming milk, stitching tiny clothes for the unexpected baby.

"She will. Ana will see to it," Rosie replied.

They worked in tandem, caring for Lillian until Ana's return at noon. They would spend the afternoon together caring for the baby, and then Izzy and Rosie would return to their homes.

Later that evening, Izzy felt the familiar prick of unease as Albert's question cut through the quiet.

"Isabelle, why are you never here when I return?" Albert's voice was tinged with confusion and a hint of frustration, his gaze searching hers for an answer.

"Ana needs help with Lillian," Izzy said finally. "Rosie and I…we share the burden."

Albert's brows furrowed. He was used to managing everyone and everything in his life. And his wife has been helping her sister with a baby, he'd barely known existed? How was that even possible?

"Share the burden," he said. "Is she still helping William in the infirmary every morning? I can't see another reason for her to need someone to mind her child."

"She is. Every morning. He keeps telling her what a wonderful nurse she is." She shrugged. "Rosie and I enjoy our time with the baby. We don't mind helping. But then I'm not home as much, but to be honest, I didn't think you cared."

He froze for a moment. "Why would you think that?"

"You're not the warmest person I've ever known."

Albert frowned. "I hope that doesn't make you doubt your place in my life."

"Of course, it does," she said softly. She didn't know where she found the will to walk away from him, but it came from somewhere deep within. She didn't need him to see how very vulnerable she was.

ALBERT LOOKED THROUGH the meager supply of brushes the general store had in stock. He would probably have to place a special order because they never had the brushes he needed in stock when he needed them. Thankfully, they had a catalog he could look through and choose his brushes from.

"Albert?"

He turned at the sound of his name, finding the kindly face of Dr. William Mercer peering at him from the end of the aisle.

"William," he greeted. "I trust all is well with you and Ana? And the baby?"

"Yes. It's been hard for us to learn the baby's rhythms, and I'm afraid Ana does more than her share of the work." William replied with a nod. "And congratulations! I know you and Izzy are excited!"

Albert frowned, having no idea what his friend was talking about. "Congratulations? For what may I ask?"

William laughed, shaking his head. "For the baby!"

Albert blinked at the other man for a moment. Izzy was expecting? "Thank you, William," he managed.

Albert walked home mechanically. He was surprised at his wife's silence. Why hadn't Izzy told him? It made no sense to him. They were happy. Why wouldn't she want him to know she was expecting?

The question gnawed at him. Was it fear that silenced her, or doubt?

When he reached his front porch, he sat down abruptly on the porch swing. Inside, he imagined Izzy bustling about her day, her secret nestled deep within her, growing alongside their unborn child. How could she hide this from him? She knew he wanted children!

After what could have been hours or mere seconds, he stood, walking into the house and finding his wife in the kitchen with Martha. "Izzy," he began, "we need to talk."

Her movements ceased, and she turned to face him. In her eyes, he searched for an anchor, a lifeline amidst the turbulent seas he found himself in.

"Of course, Albert," she answered. "What is it?"

Instead of answering immediately, Albert took her hand and pulled her from the kitchen into the parlor.

Chapter Ten

With the weight of Albert's gaze upon her, Izzy turned, meeting eyes that seemed to search her soul.

"Isabelle," he began, his voice laced with confusion, "what is this I hear about...a baby?"

For a moment, time stood still, and Izzy stared at him, bewildered. How had he found out?

She drew a ragged breath, her eyes not leaving his. "Yes, Albert," she confessed, "I'm expecting."

He stepped back as if struck, his hand reaching out as though to grasp something that was no longer there.

"Why, Izzy?" he asked, the hurt evident in his voice. "Why didn't you tell me?"

Izzy's throat tightened, and she fought back the moisture threatening to spill from her eyes. "I needed to know," she said, "how you truly felt about me, Albert. Before I added another life into the equation of our...arrangement."

"Izzy," he said, his voice low and edged with disbelief, "how could you ever doubt my feelings for you?"

She didn't know how to respond to that. How could she not doubt his feelings for her? He'd never told her how he felt. Was she supposed to simply know?

"Your words," she said, "they were not the same as...as your touch, Albert. At night—" She faltered, her resolve crumbling beneath the pressure of his scrutiny.

He drew in a sharp breath, the sound harsh in the stillness. "Words," he asked. "What use are words when every day I've built a life around you? Can't you see it, Izzy? Everything I do...it is all for us."

"Us?" she asked. It seemed so strange that he spoke as if they were in love when she knew he didn't feel that way about her. If he did, why hadn't he told her?

"Us," he said.

For a moment, neither moved, the distance between them stretching into an impassable chasm. Then, without another word, Albert turned on his heel.

The door closed behind him with a finality that echoed through the empty room. Izzy stood motionless, watching the space where he had been, her heart aching with a sense of loss she couldn't name.

Albert walked, each step carrying him further from home. His gaze roamed listlessly until it was caught by a familiar sight—a rough-hewn wooden swing hanging from the stout arm of an old oak tree at the edge of town. He had once spent an afternoon with Izzy, picnicking near the swing and he had pushed her on it, entranced by her laughter, a sound he hadn't heard nearly enough.

He collapsed onto it, the ropes groaning under his weight. His eyes traced the empty spaces between the stars, seeking answers in their silent judgment. Time stretched taut around him, minutes bleeding into hours.

There, in the stillness, Albert grappled with the truth of his failings. The stark reality was that although his heart had been full, his actions had been empty. He could see where he was at fault, and he despised himself for it.

"Damn," he muttered. "Damn my silence."

Izzy pushed a morsel of food around her plate, her appetite as absent as the man whose chair sat vacant across from her.

Her thoughts churned as she wondered where Albert had gone and if and when he would be home. She nibbled on a piece of bread, the dry crust scraping against her throat with each forced swallow.

The creak of the front door broke the silence, announcing Albert's return. Izzy bowed her head for a moment, caught between relief and dread. She rose from the table as she braced herself for his reaction.

"Albert," she began, her voice barely above a whisper, "I'm—I'm sorry." She searched his face for any sign of warmth, but there was none to be seen.

"Every night," she continued, her words tumbling out in an anxious rush, "you come to me, and I feel...wanted. But during the day, it's like you're a different person. It's as if I don't exist until the shadows fall again." Her hands twisted the fabric of her skirt, seeking solace in the tactile distraction from the pain that constricted her chest.

"Is that all I am to you, Albert? A convenient arrangement for the nights?" The question hung between them, heavy and accusing.

His eyes finally met hers, and in them, she saw a glimmer of the conflict that raged within him. "I—," he started, then stopped, as if the words were foreign on his tongue.

"Isabelle," he began, his voice a low rumble of emotion. "I have loved you from the very moment I laid eyes upon you."

She looked up at him, her eyes wide. The confession was a soft blow, disarming and raw. She had been a stranger to him, a name on a paper, a solution to the empty space beside him at the table, in the bed, in his life. But love?

"Love?" Her voice was a whisper.

"Yes, love. I never intended for us to be...more than what was necessary. A physical relationship wasn't part of the plan with my mail-order bride."

"Albert," she replied, the strength in her voice surprising her, "I have loved you since the first week we were married."

His reaction was immediate, the tension in his shoulders softening. "Truly?" he asked.

"Truly," she said, walking slowly toward him at first and gaining speed until she was in front of him.

He wrapped his arms around her, pulling her close. When his lips found hers, she knew that he'd told her the truth. It was in his kiss. All of the love she'd ever dreamed of feeling was right there in his kiss.

Epilogue

Albert and Izzy sat side by side on the wooden porch, the creaking of the swing a soft counterpoint to the chorus of crickets.

"Your work," Izzy said, "the clients coming tomorrow...you've done well. You know I would be content if you never sold a piece because we have all we need."

"I know. And without you," he replied, his gaze fixed on the horizon, "none of it would hold meaning."

She rested her head on his shoulder, feeling the weight of the world they had built together.

"I love you," he whispered, the declaration a sacred offering laid bare in the night's embrace.

And there, beneath the indifferent canvas of stars, they held each other, two kindred spirits navigating the vast, uncharted expanse of the future, bound by love.

Izzy's hands rested atop the swell of her belly, the fabric of her dress stretched taut over new life within. She watched as her twin girls, two cherubic mirrors of mischief, played with Ana's twin boys and little Lillian. The children's laughter never ceased to make her smile.

"Hard to believe they're almost the same age," Ana said, her voice tinged with the weariness that comes from carrying yet another child. "Nine months apart. All five of them!"

"And now the next three—and hopefully three total—will be here in another five months. Sometimes I wish Rosie had a baby with the twins, but it wasn't her time."

Rosie stepped into view. The early stages of pregnancy were evident in her stance, a subtle shift to accommodate the burgeoning weight.

"Seems this porch is becoming a cradle of sorts," Rosie said.

"I like that idea. All of our babies playing together as we played together at their ages," Ana said. "I wonder why Mother never had more children after the three of us."

Izzy shook her head. "We may never know."

"It's not like Father is going to tell us anything," Rosie said, shaking her head.

The clinking of metal echoed across the yard, punctuated by masculine laughter and the dull thud of horseshoes. Albert and his friends were lost in their game, a small world unto themselves, a tableau of camaraderie and competition that seemed almost childlike in its simplicity.

Izzy watched from a distance, her fingers absently tracing the swell of her belly, the life within a secret murmur against her skin. Tomorrow, a group of men would come to purchase some of Albert's paintings.

After her sisters were gone, taking their husbands and Ana taking all three of her children, Izzy looked down at her daughters, sleeping in their shared bed. They looked so angelic and perfect. "It's so strange that my twins are identical and Ana's aren't," Izzy said softly as she felt rather than heard Albert walk up behind her.

"Don't you mean *our* twins?" he asked, smiling. "I wasn't aware you'd begun making children on your own."

She laughed softly, turning to face him. "Our children then. It just feels that they are more mine because they are twins. I know that's odd."

"It is, but I understand it. And I now understand why you felt the need to dress like your sisters for that party we had so long ago. Our girls don't seem to like it when they're not dressed alike."

Izzy laughed, kissing his chin. "Maybe they don't. I know Ana, Rosie, and I hated when we weren't allowed to dress alike."

He frowned. "You weren't allowed to?"

"At times," Izzy said sighing. "Father didn't think we should always look alike. I never understood why."

"I think there are many things about your father we'll always have to wonder about."

She rested her cheek on his shoulder. "I love our life together, Albert. I love that you paint and are no longer a businessman. I wish your parents would come back so they could see you now, still successful, but in a different way."

He shook his head. "I don't need them to. I got my father's approval of my business acumen, and that's all I really cared about. I like having more time to spend with you and the girls."

"I hope this one is a boy," Izzy said, resting her hand atop her burgeoning belly. "You won't be angry if it's another girl?"

"As long as she's perfect and just like you, I would be thrilled." He took her hand and led her from the nursery. "Boy or girl doesn't matter to me. As long as you're their mother."

She chuckled. "I hope I am. Otherwise, I've swallowed a watermelon seed or something."